Horse Camp

Horse Camp

Nicole Helget and Nate LeBoutillier

EGMONT
USA
New York

EGMONT

We bring stories to life

First published by Egmont USA, 2012
443 Park Avenue South, Suite 806
New York, NY 10016

Copyright © Nicole Helget and Nate LeBoutillier, 2012
All rights reserved.

1 3 5 7 9 8 6 4 2

www.egmontusa.com
www.nateandnicole.com
Book design: ARLENE SCHLEIFER GOLDBERG

Library of Congress Cataloging-in-Publication Data
Helget, Nicole Lea, 1976-
Horse camp : a novel / by Nicole Helget and Nate LeBoutillier.
p. cm.
Summary: When their mom sends them to their uncle's farm for the summer,
twins Percy and Penny are excited to spend the summer riding horses,
until they discover it's a pig farm.
ISBN 978-1-60684-351-2 (hardcover) -- ISBN 978-1-60684-352-9 (e-book)
[1. Farm life--Minnesota--Fiction. 2. Brothers and sisters--Fiction. 3. Twins--
Fiction. 4. Uncles--Fiction. 5. Family problems--Fiction. 6. Missionaries--Fiction.
7. Minnesota--Fiction.] I. LeBoutillier, Nate. II. Title.
PZ7.H374085Hor 2012
[Fic]--dc23
2011038114

Printed in the United States of America

For Isabella and Mitchell and Phillip

Table of Contents

Horse Camp

Chapter 1
Percy and the Pigs

Uncle Stretch sits on a wooden three-legged stool in the corner of the pig barn, holding a knife in one hand. He is not what I would call a good role model.

The pig barn on Uncle Stretch's farm in Minnesota is my least favorite place in the world. It smells like a garbage dump, and it's packed with about fifty grunting, squealing pigs of all sizes. Outside the pig barn isn't much of an improvement, with chickens running about in the farmyard and a bunch of tractors and other farming machines all over the place. It is not what I would call the sweetest place to spend your summer, which I can already tell, having been here a whole week.

Uncle Stretch points the knife at a pack of smaller pigs trying to stick their noses through a crack in one of the wooden boards holding them inside the pen. "Get me one of those," he says.

"Are you crazy?" I say, my arms rising in protest like a professional football player's when he's forced to argue with refs who call unfair penalties.

Uncle Stretch scrapes the blade of the knife on his boot heel. He lifts one eyebrow at me. "I said, go get me one, Perseus."

"How come Penny doesn't have to help?" I ask, even though if I know one thing about my twin sister, it's that she can't deal with dirt and germs, which happen to be about 99 percent of what pigs are made.

"She's got her own chores in the house," says Uncle Stretch.

"C'mon!" I say. "This is the most disgusting thing in history."

Uncle Stretch twirls the knife in his hand, then points it at the pack of pigs. "I ain't gonna tell you again, young gun," he says.

When our parents sent us here to Uncle Stretch's farm, they called it Horse Camp. *Oh, you'll have a great time at Horse Camp. Yeah, Stretch always has bunches of horses out on his farm. You can ride and ride and ride. It's the best place in the world for a kid to spend the summer. You'll love it! And if you don't, remember it's just temporary until we get this mess all sorted out.* All I can say to that is, *Yeah, right.*

Stretch has got just two horses now—one a worn-down steed named Bernie, who looks like he was in the Civil War, and the other a mean mare named Brenda, who would rather bite your whole hand off than eat the carrot you're holding out for her. I wouldn't dream of riding those two creatures even if the world was on fire, and I had to get away from it fast. Horse Camp? Ha. More like Annoying Camp. Or Foolish Camp. Or Camp for Crazy People and Animals.

I walk over to the pack of pigs. They ignore me and keep nosing at the crack in the boards. The pigs I've seen around here act pretty dumb. I saw one eating a paper feed bag yesterday. Another was eating something smelly and steaming that I don't even want to talk about. All the pigs in the group I'm approaching now are smaller, not quite grown-up. They probably weigh as much as a little kid, like a two-year-old. I used to have to carry around my brother, Pauly, when he was two, so I know what I'm talking about.

I step into the middle of the pack and reach down to pick one up. It squeals and takes off. *Whatever.* I reach for another one, but it squeals and dashes after its friend. *Stupid, filthy animals.* The other pigs in the pack have stopped nosing the crack and are nosing my knees now. I look over at Uncle Stretch and throw my hands up again. He points the knife at me and shakes it. *What the heck is that supposed to mean?*

I reach down a third time and get ahold of a leg. The pig whose leg I've got starts screaming like I'm killing it, and the rest of the pack runs away, but I hold on. The pig pulls and tries to run with only three legs on the ground. I yank on the leg and try to drag it, but the screams the pig lets out make me feel sorry for it. Maybe I'm breaking its leg. I try to switch my grip to its belly, and I get it about a foot off the ground when it's like a bolt of lightning hits the pig and it jolts and all its legs run in the air at once. Suddenly, a jet of yellow liquid comes out of the pig's butt and lands all over the sleeve of my Minnesota Vikings sweatshirt.

"Jeez!" I say, flinging the thing away from me and shaking my sleeve. My mom and dad would kill me for taking the Lord's name in vain, but what's on my sleeve looks and smells so evil that I have to say something. The little devil runs off with its pack of buddies.

I walk over to Uncle Stretch, holding my arm out straight like it's not a part of me. I stand in front of him and stare.

"Well?" he says. "What happened?"

"Uh, look what that pig did to my arm!" I say. "He probably ruined my sweatshirt."

"The Vikings have always stunk," he says, pointing

the knife at the purple helmet with the white horns on it in the middle of my chest. He smiles.

I don't laugh at his dumb joke. "I'm leaving," I say. I turn and take a couple of steps before I feel a yanking on my neck. Uncle Stretch pulls me back in front of him by my sweatshirt hood.

"Ouch!" I say. "You're choking me!" I rub my neck.

"You need to go get me one of those pigs now," he says, not smiling at all. I wonder if he'd beat me up if I try taking off again. Uncle Stretch's eyes are real squinty, like my mom's when she's mad at us. It makes sense, since they're brother and sister.

"I can't get 'em," I say. "They're too . . ." I want to say *fast*, but that would mean I think they're faster than me, and I don't think that's true. "They're too gross," I say.

"They're pigs," says Uncle Stretch.

He's got a point, so I just say, "I've never done this before."

Uncle Stretch looks at my sweatshirt. "You like football, right?" he says.

"Yeah."

"You ever play it, or just watch on TV?"

"I play it all the time," I say, offended.

"You ever tackle anybody?" he asks.

"Millions of times," I say.

Uncle Stretch points his knife again. It's aimed at a

little pig wandering off by itself. "Go tackle that one," he says. "And then bring him over to me."

"What if he craps on me?" I say.

"A little pig crap never hurt anyone," says Uncle Stretch. "Some even use it as an antibiotic."

I can't help but smile at that. My parents are missionaries and they never swear or say words like *crap*, at least around me. The little pig is sniffing at the ground, but it looks around and grunts when it sees me sneaking up on it. I make a mad dash and dive for it, but it jumps out of the way. I pound the dirt like a cornerback might when he just misses an interception. Then I get up, dust off my pants, and start after the pig. It's joined the pack again, and I figure if I dive into the middle of the pack, I'll land on at least one pig. I let out a big yell and go flying through the air. *BAM!* I land on parts of at least three pigs and suddenly am surrounded by crazy squeals and flying hooves. One of the hooves is coming straight for my eyes. I jerk my head back, but the hoof clips me, like a knife on the chin. The pain is instant and sharp, and when I touch my chin, I feel something slimy dripping into my fingers. I pull my fingers away, and they're red. Blood!

I can't help it. The tears start to come. I get up with my head down and limp over to Uncle Stretch, cupping my chin with my hand.

"Let me see," he says, and takes my hand away to look. He squints one eye at me and says, "That's a deep one."

His words scare me. More tears. I try to make them stop because I'm embarrassed—embarrassed that a pig did this to me, and embarrassed that Uncle Stretch saw the whole thing. I could have a scar! Because of a pig!

"How far's the hospital?" I say.

Uncle Stretch ignores me and opens a cabinet on the wall. He takes out a bottle of something and grabs a roll of duct tape.

"What're you gonna do with that?" I say, but I think I already know.

"C'mere," says Uncle Stretch.

I really have no choice. I take a step toward Uncle Stretch, and he has me kneel and lay my head across his lap. He smears some stuff on my chin, and it stings. Then he unrolls a length of duct tape with a ripping sound.

I try to stop crying, but I'm truly in pain here. I want my mom or dad, not Uncle Stretch.

"Hold still," says Uncle Stretch. "Think about something else for a minute. This is gonna pinch a little bit."

I try to think of something else, but it's hard. I try to think of football, or other places I wish I could've gone this summer instead of Uncle Stretch's Horse Camp, but mostly I just try to stop crying. Uncle Stretch rips the duct tape into strips and presses them to my chin. I finally think of something else. "What were you gonna do with that knife if I brought you a pig?"

"Castration," says Uncle Stretch.

I'm pretty sure I know what that means, but if I'm right, I don't want to think about it.

Chapter 2

PENNY AND GOD'S CHALLENGES

Dear Diary,

You'd expect a girl my age to be exploring her deepest thoughts on a laptop or maybe texting, Facebooking, or Tweeting everyone about the horrible, really awful, and unfair tragedies that have befallen her these past few weeks. Instead, I write these thoughts by hand in a spiral notebook like people used to do centuries ago. If I ever require emergency surgery for carpal tunnel syndrome, here's who to blame: Uncle Stretch!

Here's why:

Me: I can't stand it here. This farm is like the eighteenth century but way worse! (It's totally worse.

The water has a rusty taste, and all the meat used to be animals on the farm. But I was trying to be calm.)

Uncle Stretch: (Raises his eyebrows in confusion, as though he doesn't even know what century we're in.) What are you talking about?

Me: Hello? Are you listening to me? Is there a wireless signal anywhere near here?

Stretch: (Grimacing, since his idea of living is running this farm as old-fashioned as possible. He acts as though he wants to be Charles Ingalls from the Little House books. He expects me to behave like Half-Pint, who would have been delirious with happiness over receiving one orange for Christmas or going on a walk with an old person or wearing a hand-me-down.) Are you always this dramatic?

Me: You know, wireless, like, for the Internet? Don't you have a cell phone or something? Where's the phone reception? Do you have a cell phone tower around here?

Stretch: (Taking a lazy bite from an apple he picked from his own tree. The apple probably has a worm in it because Uncle Stretch's whole farm is organic, which means he doesn't use pesticide. All his fruits are probably writhing with worms and bugs. Using the apple to gesture toward the wall.) I have the rotary over there that you can use to talk to your mom when she calls.

Me: THAT'S your actual phone? I thought that was an antique for decoration. No way! How am I supposed to talk to my dad? What if he's trying to call my cell phone, but it's not getting through? (Holding up my dead, nonreceptive cell phone for extra effect.)

Stretch: He's not calling. Won't call. (Taking another bite and staring out the window to his fields, which have lots of weeds he makes us pull by hand.) You may as well throw that celly-phone in the junk drawer.

Me: (Clutching my cell phone to my chest.) It's called a *cell* phone. I can't live here. I have to have access to the outside world!

Stretch: Snap out of it. I don't like hysterics. (Picking up the notebook from the counter near the phone and handing it to me.) Here. You can pour your heart out in there if that's what you need to do to keep from flapping around like a chicken with its head cut off.

Me: This notebook smells like horse feed.

Stretch: When you're done writing in that thing, meet me in the end rows with a hoe. Gotta get them cockleburs out of the field before they choke out the beets.

Even in the poorest countries I've lived in, Internet and phone service were readily available, and we always lived in the nicest house in the town or village because everyone respected my dad. He was kind of like a celebrity to them because he was bringing the good news about Jesus and being saved. And he needed the Internet to podcast his sermons and take online donations. Uncle Stretch's farm is not at all what I'm used to. Even though it's in the state of Minnesota, the heart of civilized America, it's the most remote, most lonely place I've ever lived. But I'm going to do my best to endure this sacrifice and pray that the Lord makes my will strong.

Anyway, here's some information about me: I am Penelope Rachel Pribyl. I am almost thirteen years old. I am a Christian. I am five foot two and getting taller. I have long brown hair, which is not at all frizzy like some girls' hair. When we lived in Africa, the little kids there used to try and touch my long hair all the time, because they thought it was so pretty. I have brownish-green eyes that have little flecks of yellow in them. I have a twin brother, Perseus. I have a little brother, Pauly, who is adopted from the Philippines. I have been all over the world, including the continents of Africa, South America, and Asia. I have been mostly homeschooled and test far above my age group. I don't have a best friend, though I have many acquaintances. I have never been in love. I want to minister to the poor and lost when I grow up, just like my dad.

Dad always preaches that the disintegration of the nuclear family is at the heart of all the world's troubles and sins, and I couldn't agree more! It's just not right that my own nuclear family is disintegrating! In Africa, Dad mostly preached to the women and children. (The men never came to church unless they wanted to collect their wives to come home and make them something to eat.) They rarely seemed to care about Jesus or being saved. Most of the time, they just came because Mom would give their kids free checkups, medicines, and immunizations. She had a brief career as a registered nurse before she met Dad and got involved in his ministry. She has a college degree and everything.

But when your husband is called by God to be a minister, you're supposed to go along with it and be a good pastor's wife. Dad said that Mom should stop running around like a feminist and get busy worrying about the spirits of the parishioners rather than their little aches and pains. But Mom just couldn't stop herself from nursing, no matter what Dad or us or even God wanted. She nursed wherever we went and never seemed very interested in being a dutiful pastor's wife.

We left Africa after a short time because it was just

so obvious that the people there didn't care about the disintegration of the nuclear family, and they wouldn't donate any money to build a decent church building. I got really sick once, too, and Mom had to sit by my bed day and night with cool washcloths and give me droppers of medicine. Finally, one night, Dad said a prayer of healing over me, and the very next day, I sat up and felt a lot better. It was a miracle! I, for one, believe in miracles.

After moving here and there, we lived in the Philippines for a little while. That was my favorite place. The Philippine government has laws against divorce, for one thing. Married people can't just wake up one morning and get a divorce, like they can here. And the people there are very, very concerned about keeping the nuclear family together. They also have very pretty beaches and water. They have good food, not like roasted goat or yams, which is all they seemed to eat in Africa unless you order special food from America. That's what we did most of the time because Dad said the native food gave him gas.

And the Philippines is where we picked up Pauly, our little brother. I love him like crazy, and, not to brag or anything, but I've basically raised him these past three years. Pauly's got the best nature of any kid I've ever met, and I can't understand how any mother could've abandoned him. But that's exactly what

happened. One morning, Mom opened up the front
door to sweep the dirt outside. She looked down and
saw him sitting on our doorstep, with a note pinned to
his shirt:

> I am very sick. And my husband is a very
> bad and abusive man. Please look after this
> child. I love him but cannot allow him to grow
> up in such a house. I heard you are a very
> good mother and will love him as your own
> baby.

Pauly looked up at Mom and smiled, and she was
hooked. To look at him, you instantly know why. He's
really adorable. I sometimes wish I had big dark brown
eyes and long black lashes like his, but then I
remember it's a sin to be envious, and I'm just happy
that I can enjoy those features on Pauly.

I used to be Pauly's favorite person by far, but since
we've come here, Stretch is the one Pauly follows
around all day long, from the house to the barn to the
pigpens to the field. Stretch lets him feed the horses
and even sets him on top of the pigs. He gives him
rides on the tractor and makes him homemade
pancakes every morning because they're Pauly's
favorite food. Stretch lets Pauly pour on his own
syrup and doesn't monitor him when he brushes his

teeth, which is not how a responsible adult should act.

Stretch's farm is located on a gravel road at least ten miles from the nearest town, so we're miles from people who need to be saved by God's grace. Compared to the exotic places we've lived, this area is quite boring. The town has two small schools (one regular, one Catholic), a gas station/bait shop (LIVE NIGHT CRAWLERS HALF OFF!), and a café run by a woman who also operates a beauty parlor in the same building. Stretch goes there often to buy people's hair from her. He says he uses the hair balls to repel deer and rabbits from his young vegetable plants. I think he just goes to the beauty parlor because he likes to ogle the breasts of one of the beauticians. She seems pretty nice, but she does flirt with Stretch.

The town also has a farm equipment dealer, a grain elevator, a small medical clinic, a funeral home (RESPECTFUL QUALITY THROUGH CARING COMFORT—BURY YOUR LOVED ONE WITH DIGNITY), an American Legion, and a butcher shop where Stretch sometimes brings his animals for slaughter. The town is so small it doesn't even have a shopping center or a movie theater, though it does have a library, which has a couple of computers with Internet service. A nun named Sister Alice is the librarian, and she's not very nice, but she did used to be a missionary, like my parents, so she can be pretty interesting to talk to if she's not crabby. I think she's bitter about having to wear that hot and itchy habit all day.

I try to be good and nonjudgmental and righteous in the Lord's eyes. I do not like how my mom has ruined our family. I do not like how she embarrassed my dad and his church and all of us. You might think I'd be really, really angry at her, but I'm not. I'm just very, very disappointed. I do not like staying at Stretch's farm while she's on trial for distributing prescription drugs without a license to people who couldn't afford them.

When Mom said she was sending us to an uncle we'd never even known, we were scared, so she tried to make it sound better by referring to Stretch's place as *Horse Camp*, since she said Stretch had always had a lot of horses, and we'd probably be riding around every day like regular cowboys. My mom also tried to make the farm sound more appealing by telling me it was an organic farm, and that I'd be learning a lot about self-sustainability and going green. I've been to Bible camp and Jesus camp and the Little Saviors Camp and youth ministries camp, where they always had a point or a message. There's no point to us being at Horse Camp. What's more, the horses are very dysfunctional, and I, for one, would never ride them, for the simple fact that they are both clearly safety hazards. As far as the *organic farm* goes, it's much dirtier than I imagined it would be, and I have a hard time dealing with things like manure.

So far, I just keep myself busy by cleaning up the house. One thing about me is that I'm very, very neat and clean. You can't be too careful about germs, which are everywhere! Bleach and rubbing alcohol and hand sanitizer are very important to me. I also think personal hygiene is *very* important. I've seen how little parasites and germs and diseases can make a person really sick and even kill him or her.

Percy takes a shower only once or twice a week, which nearly drives me crazy. But since he's my age, I can't really do anything about it other than tell him he smells like rancid chicken soup and show him photos of awful skin diseases to scare him. I'm sure he'll get an infection from that cut on his chin that Stretch just duct-taped together.

One good thing about being here and being perpetually B-O-R-E-D is that I have plenty of time to reflect and pray. I've been praying for a long time for the gift of tongues or the gift of healing like Dad has, but so far, it's not happening. I don't know why the Lord won't give me a sign that I'm in His grace! It's very frustrating. I love Jesus so much, and I try to be grateful for the gifts He's given me, one of which is a very good memory. I remember everything and can tell you exactly how Mom ruined our family. A couple of days before we kids were sent here, I overheard Mom and Dad fighting.

Mom: Allen, cut the bull! (Can you imagine saying that to a minister?!) You may fool the parishioners, but I'm not buying the Holy-Rolling act anymore. I'm through!

Dad: Danielle, without me you cannot survive financially or spiritually. You are an empty woman.

Mom: Who do you think you're talking to? I'm taking the kids, and I'm getting out of this crazy life.

Dad: Neither the children, nor you are going anywhere.

Mom: What's that supposed to mean?

Dad: No court will give the children to an unstable criminal like yourself. If you want your children, you'll stay right where you are and take your proper place in the front pew and at my side when I need you. You're the one on trial. Remember? You need me.

Mom: I can't, Allen! I don't believe the things you say. I don't like what you stand for. You're a poser, a faker, and I'm not going along with it anymore. You're taking money from people who've worked hard to earn it.

Dad: The money is donated for the church.

Mom: (Interrupting, *again*.) But you are the church!

The church's success is your success. The money is for you, for your ego. The bigger the church, the bigger the man.

Dad: Well, you've not complained one bit about the life we've lived.

Mom: Well, I'm complaining now. Consider this an official complaint.

And on and on it went. Mom told Dad that she questioned his very belief in his own religion. She called him a money-hungry poser about a hundred and four times. She said he just watches televangelists and then copies basically everything they do, particularly their faith-healing techniques. Then she started shaking and raising her arms and mocking him in a low, rumbly voice like Dad uses: *Do you believe? Do you believe you can be healed? If you believe in Him, you will be healed!* Dad got really mad and looked up to the ceiling, and I thought he was going to call down some punishment on Mom. But he didn't. He's a very forgiving kind of person. He's a servant of God, after all, and how can you argue with that? But then he said this:

Dad: Well then, I guess you won't mind if I don't post bail for you. You can sit in jail while you wait for your trial. Come to think of it, I don't think it would be right to use the church's money to bail out a criminal like yourself.

Mom: You'd leave the kids without their mother just to prove a point?

Dad: They're better off without you, anyway. You're a bad influence.

Mom: You wouldn't dare. Who's going to care for them?

Dad: That's your problem. I've got to catch a flight out of here in the morning, to set up the next church. You figure it out.

Then he left. True to his word, Dad cancelled the check on Mom's bail.

Mom likes to argue about everything. She thinks she's above the law of God and everyone else. And that's why we're here at Horse Camp without Dad and Mom while they sort out their professional and personal lives. She's gotten herself into trouble for acquiring and distributing pharmaceuticals without a license. If you think it sounds bad, that's because it is. Even though Mom is a nurse in the United States, that doesn't mean she can go to any old country and be a nurse there. They have laws! But did that stop her from helping people? No. Did that stop her from bringing prescription medications to people in Africa and the Philippines? No. Did that stop her from buying cheap generic drugs from Canada? No. Did that stop her from holding meetings with the women of the villages to talk to them about diet, health, exercise, and immunizing their children? No. Did that stop her from warning those women about big drug companies coming into their countries and using them as guinea pigs to test out their new medicines? No. Did that stop her from writing extensive editorials to all the major newspapers about how the pharmaceutical companies are using human beings in poor countries to test out their new drugs? No.

What the trial's really about is money, Mom says. She says that the big, fat drug companies are just mad that she revealed their dirty little secret, and they're making an example of her. She says, shame on them. I see her point, but *she* is the one on trial and facing prison time. *She* is the one responsible for the disintegration of our nuclear family, and *nothing's* worse than that.

Since she was arrested and sued, Mom has been in the newspapers and on TV and the Internet, and *not* in a good way. Even CNN ran a story on her arrest. Someone put it on YouTube, and most of the comments below the video are very disparaging. Dad got really mad at her for embarrassing him and threatening his authority in the new church he's been working on. The week before we kids got sent here, he even gave a sermon about how good people sometimes have to cut the ties with bad influences and evil forces in their lives. Mom sat straight and calm in the front row like she always does, but her face turned from tan to white. Dad was pretty harsh, but she shouldn't have been doing things that were illegal, for goodness' sake. He does have to think about his flock and the way things look. I mean, that's just the nature of his calling. Anyway, a couple of days later, he filed for divorce. I was pretty surprised, but now I can see that he's just trying to teach her a lesson and doesn't really want to divorce her.

You might think I'd be really upset about all of this, but I'm not. Dad is only trying to scare Mom straight. Being here seems like a sort of joke, and I don't plan on having to stay for more than another week. Two weeks, tops.

DEAR OKONKWO,

EVEN THOUGH I AM PERSONALLY EXPERIENCING MANY PERSONAL TRAGEDIES IN MY OWN LIFE, ONE OF WHICH IS THAT I NO LONGER HAVE ACCESS TO THE INTERNET, I AM HAPPY TO HELP YOU. BEFORE I LOST ALL ACCESS TO THE OUTSIDE WORLD, I SAW AN AD FOR CHRISTIANS SAVING HUNGRY CHILDREN AND DECIDED TO ADOPT YOU. WHILE I DON'T HAVE A

LOT OF MONEY, I CAN SPARE SOME AND AM
SENDING $5 WITH THIS LETTER. I'VE SEEN
MANY, MANY COMMERCIALS ON TELEVISION
FOR CHRISTIANS SAVING HUNGRY CHILDREN
AND EVEN LIVED IN AFRICA FOR A WHILE, SO I
KNOW YOUR NEED IS GREAT AND URGENT. I
ALSO KNOW HOW THIS ADOPTION THING
WORKS, AND I MUST SAY YOU ARE ONE LUCKY
YOUNG MAN. I WILL BE SENDING YOU MONEY
AND THE WORD OF GOD IN THE MAIL ONCE A
MONTH FROM NOW ON, AND I MAY MAKE A
USEFUL SUGGESTION OR TWO TO HELP YOU
LIVE A BETTER LIFE.

REMEMBER THAT EVEN THOUGH YOU ARE
POOR, YOU ARE A CHILD OF GOD, AND JESUS
LOVES YOU.

YOURS TRULY IN CHRIST,
PENELOPE PRIBYL

Chapter 3
Percy in the Granary

I'M IN BED, drawing by the light of my flashlight when I feel a *whump*—Pauly kicking the underside of my mattress through the metal bars from the bunk below. Another *whump* comes, and then another.

"Pauly, knock it off!" I whisper.

Whump, whump.

"Pauly!"

"Light off, P.P.," says Pauly.

"Not yet," I say to him. "I'm not finished, you jerk."

Even though Pauly isn't my real brother, he annoys me like a real brother. Everybody thinks he's so cute. Penny always sides with him, and so do Mom and Dad, usually, but he's not as cute as he looks. Even though I'm over twice his age, he starts about every fight we have.

Whump, whump, whump. The last *whump* is so hard that I go flying up like a horse bucked me, which would never actually happen around here because no kids can even ride the worthless horses.

"Pauly!" I hiss.

"Tohn yoh light off, Pohcy," says Pauly, loudly.

Pauly has an *R* problem. I'd make more fun of him for it, except I had it, too, until second grade, even though we're not related. As a result of this, he usually avoids *R* words. Like, instead of calling something a *car* because it will sound like *cow*, he'll call it *you know, that thing with wheels*. It's also one reason he often calls me by my initials, P.P., instead of Percy. The other reason, of course, is that P.P. sounds like, you know, number one. Pauly talks as little as possible, maybe because of the *R* thing or because he's still getting used to the American English accent instead of his native accent or because he just doesn't feel like it. He's a man of action, as my dad says. Problem is, most of his actions annoy me.

Our door cracks open, and Penny sticks her head in. "Uncle Stretch said lights out!" she says. "You need to respect his word, Percy."

Uncle Stretch did say we're supposed to have lights out, but I really want to finish this drawing I started two days ago. It's a freehand copy of a picture of Perseus, the Greek warrior guy I was named after, although I prefer to be called Percy. It's from a book of Greek mythology that I was given by some pastor friend of my parents. In the picture, Perseus defends himself from an attacking soldier.

I've barely had any time at all to draw since Uncle Stretch decided on working me to death here at Horse Camp. Instead of drawing, I have to feed pigs and cows and shovel junk around and power-wash things. It's exhausting. I will never be a farmer when I grow up.

"I'm busy, Penny," I say, "so why don't you go back to your own room and mind your own business, okay?"

"I rebuke that spirit of rebellion rearing its ugly, horned head in you, Percy," says Penny. "I rebuke it in the name of Jesus."

It frustrates me that Penny's always trying to talk like Dad. Ever since we got to Horse Camp, it seems she's trying to *be* Dad or Mom. "Go rebuke yourself," I say back, loud. My voice gets loud when I'm excited.

There's a pounding on the walls downstairs followed by Uncle Stretch's voice yelling, "What's going on up there?"

Penny's eyes get big. "We have to obey Uncle Stretch," she says.

"He can go to heck," I say. "And you can go back to your room."

27

Penny covers her mouth like she's shocked, but she's just a big faker. She turns to scamper out of the room, but first she says, "I'll pray for you, Percy."

I try to get back to work on the drawing, doing some shading on the muscles of Perseus's arm, which holds a big sword. I wish I had a sword, sometimes. A guy we knew once in Zambia had one.

Just as I really begin to concentrate, Pauly kicks at my mattress again, making me scribble a jagged line across my picture.

"Dang you, Pauly!" I say, and I swing my pillow over the side, under the bed, and nail him. He kicks my mattress again, and I almost fly off.

"Pauly, stop it now!" I say. "You're going to hurt somebody."

He *whumps* again, and I have to hang on to the rail to keep from falling out of the bed.

"You little idiot!" I say, and swing my pillow under again. The overhead light snaps on as my pillow catches Pauly, and he thumps backwards into the wall. Hard.

Before I know it, Pauly's crying, and Uncle Stretch is yanking me out of bed by my neck, throwing me to my feet, and kicking me in the butt. He wears an old-fashioned nightgown that looks like a woman's. I'm caught between howling in self-defense and laughing. A weird sound comes out of my mouth.

"You should pick on somebody your own size," says Uncle Stretch.

"There *is* nobody else my size around here," I say, rubbing my butt. "And thanks for breaking my tail-bone."

"You got a smart mouth, Son," says Uncle Stretch. He goes over to Pauly and sits on the bottom bunk. "Stop crying now, kiddo," he says to Pauly, who's rubbing his head. "You're fine now. Stop crying, I said. Be a man."

Pauly stops crying instantly, like somebody turned off a faucet. He even smiles a little.

"Well, I'm not your son," I say. I don't know exactly what makes me say it. Maybe Uncle Stretch kicking me. Maybe the fact that Pauly listens to Uncle Stretch like *he* is his son. Either way, I'm usually not such a smart mouth.

"What?" says Uncle Stretch.

"P.P. said he's not yoh son," says Pauly.

"I heard him," says Uncle Stretch, "I just can't believe my ears."

"Believe 'em," I say.

"That's it," says Uncle Stretch. He grabs me by the back of the neck and marches me out of the room and into the hall. Penny's standing in the doorway of her room, and we march right past her.

"Ow," I say. "You're crushing my spinal cord!"

Uncle Stretch doesn't say anything, and he doesn't let go. He just stomps us down the stairs and out the front door. It's dark out, but the air is warm.

"Where are you taking me?" I yelp.

A couple of Uncle Stretch's farm dogs run over to us and jump up at me as I walk fast, hunched over, with Uncle Stretch's eagle talon hand clamped on to my neck. I kick at one of the dogs, and Uncle Stretch stops us and jerks me straight up.

"Ow!" I say.

"You will respect all forms of life on this farm, and that includes your brother, your sister, me, yourself, and all the animals, including the dogs," he says.

I don't get a chance to respond. Uncle Stretch is ramrodding me along, and I can barely even see where we're going. We go into a small wooden building that smells like cobwebs and dead bugs and old dust. It's dark in there, and he tugs me this way and that, and suddenly we're clomping up some wooden steps.

We enter a room, and finally Uncle Stretch releases me from his death grip. I go stumbling across the floor and almost trip over something I can barely see. A big saddle. Uncle Stretch stands close to the stairs we came up, just a square hole in the floor. The moonlight through the window lights him up like a gigantic, mean, crazy, tough lumberjack. A lumberjack in a nightshirt.

I just look back at him.

We stand there for a minute or two.

"Where is this supposed to be?" I say.

Uncle Stretch says nothing. He just stands there with his arms crossed.

"I said, 'Where is this supposed to be?'"

"You will ask any and all questions with respect, or you won't ask them at all."

"Why should I respect you?" I say. "You don't care about me. You hate me."

"You don't know anything about what I think, young man."

"Well, can you just tell me where we are?"

"This is the granary."

"What?"

"The granary. We used to keep corn here years ago, and then later on, Roland and his friends fixed it up into a clubhouse. Roland used to sleep out here sometimes in the summer."

"Who's Roland?"

"My son."

"I never heard about him."

Uncle Stretch just stands there. The moon shines off his eyes.

"Where's he live now?"

"He's dead," says Uncle Stretch.

I don't know what to say to that, so I just stand there. I kick at the saddle.

"Bed's still there," says Uncle Stretch. "There's some horse blankets over in that corner." He points.

"I'm supposed to sleep out here or something?" I get a worried feeling in my gut.

"You're not sleeping in my house until you can learn respect."

"I've got respect!" I say. "I've got all kinds of respect!"

Uncle Stretch takes a step at me like he's going to go for my neck again. I flinch and back up.

"No, you don't," he says. He turns and disappears down the hole in the floor, and it's me, a saddle, an old bed, some horse blankets, and the moon.

I look around the place, but everything's mostly dark. I have to get right up to something to see it. There are a couple of posters on one wall, a couple of football guys I've never heard of, Joe Montana and Tommy Kramer. There are also some smaller pictures. I have to get really close to see, but when I do, I nearly jump back. Women in swimsuits! In one, this lady wears a swimsuit that looks as if it is made of black rubber instead of normal swimsuit material. The rubber swimsuit also looks like it was made for a one-armed person. Half of it is missing, although the lady is covering up her bare breast with her arm. She also has a diving mask up on her forehead and is sucking her finger. Looking at the way she is sucking on that finger sends a surge of blood through my body. It's too dark to see it really good, though. I'll have to remember to look at it better during the daytime.

There's an old exercise bike in one corner, and some barbell weights on the floor and other junk I can't see. Some bottles and jars sit up higher on a shelf, but I don't even want to know what's in them. Probably booze or pee or pig pee.

I go over to the bed. When I lift the blanket, a big cloud of dust scatters up and gets in my eyes and mouth. I cough for a while until the dust settles. I go over to the pile of horse blankets in the corner and lift one up, and another dust cloud rises. I hack and cough, and chuck the thing against the wall. More dust spreads out, and I have to hang out on the other side of the room for a while.

I sit on the exercise bike and put my feet on the pedals. I push them a few times before the gear gets stuck and the pedals won't go. I start hearing little creaks and clicks. I wonder how many mice or rabid raccoons or skunks live here. There are probably all sorts of wild animals waiting to take a chomp out of my leg. We'll see who the sorry one is when I wake up dead tomorrow. I hope someone sues Uncle Stretch for putting me in this situation. He'll get arrested. He can spend some time in jail then, which isn't much better than this.

I stare at the moon. I have never been so bored,

mad, tired, lonely, scared, trapped. I think about crying or sneaking back into the house, where I'm sure Penny and Pauly are happily snoring away. I don't dare.

"Where am I?" I say to myself about a hundred times. I think for a while and then say, "Why am I here?" about a hundred more.

Nobody speaks up to answer my question, not Joe Montana or Tommy Kramer, not the finger-sucking lady in the rubber swimsuit, not even me.

Chapter 4
PENNY DEFENDS HER FAITH

Dear Mom,

I'm glad to hear that you've hired a good lawyer. I really don't know what I'd do if you had to go to prison for a long, long time! Do you have any idea how embarrassing that would be!? Do you realize what that would be like for Dad and all of us? Now that I'm here, I can certainly see why Stretch couldn't give you the money for your bail and why he offered to take us kids instead. This farm doesn't look like it produces much money at all. Everything's old. And Stretch doesn't look like he has a single cent in his pocket. No wonder he couldn't help you. Now that we're here, he'll probably just use us as slave labor.

Pauly and Percy are doing all right. Actually, they

both sort of act as though they don't remember our entire family is falling apart right before our eyes! You'll be thrilled to hear, I bet, that Pauly has taken to Stretch very well. They're basically best pals. Stretch makes pancakes for Pauly every morning. Then Pauly follows Stretch around all day, working little jobs Stretch makes up for him, like pulling dandelions out of the potato field, picking slugs off the cabbage leaves, and digging for earthworms to put in the compost pile, the dirtiest job of all, which, of course, is Pauly's favorite. Wrapping worms around his fingers is his idea of heaven. He's so young and so simple. He doesn't even realize that we're not going to be the same old nuclear family ever again.

Since Pauly's adopted, he probably thinks that people get new families every now and again throughout their lives, and they just have to adjust. Do you realize how warped that is? I'm really afraid that all of this stress is going to leave him with trusting and bonding issues later in life. I've read about these Romanian orphans who grew up in state-run orphanages. They were never held or talked to and sat in wet diapers in crowded cribs all day, every day. They grew up not knowing how to love! Lots of families adopted these poor souls only to learn that the children couldn't bond and had reactive attachment disorder (I printed out some information on it and included it here, so I hope you read it!), and the families had to send them back to Romania.

I don't want that to happen to Pauly. I think you should really consider that, Mom. Was all this business with drug pedaling (that's what Dad called it once in an argument I overheard) really worth risking your children's bonding capabilities? Was it worth losing your husband? Why not just take the plea deal, say you're sorry to the court and to Dad, and get this all over with? I *know* Dad would forgive you and take you back. He even told me so. All you have to do is repent. Let's get back to normal, *please*.

When I get married, I am never, ever going to do anything that would make my husband want to divorce me. I might even move back to the Philippines so that my husband can never, ever divorce me, no matter what.

What happened to Stretch's wife? I saw a picture taken on their wedding day. You were in the picture, too. You had on a really pretty bridesmaid dress with a very silly hat. You looked happy, though, and so did Stretch. He looked much better without that dumb mustache, in my opinion.

When Stretch saw me looking at it, he barked at me and told me to quit snooping! So if he tells you I was snooping, I want you to know that I was not. I was organizing the closets. Then he told me I'm starting to look just like you did when you were young, before Dad ruined your life. I did not like that. It's not nice to pretend to be giving people a compliment and then slam them with an insult about their dad. Please have a word with him about saying bad things about Dad.

Stretch is trying to take Dad's place, and I don't like that, either! Pauly and Percy may be falling for Stretch's games, but I am not. What he's doing is called parental alienation syndrome (I've included a printout I made at the library, so you can read about it, too). Dad is a hundred times better than Stretch. Dad is a minister, and Stretch is just a dumb organic farmer whose horses don't even look like they could carry ten pounds. Anybody would agree with me. If this is a Horse Camp, then a Horse Camp is a disaster, a calamity, a fiasco, a mess, a hoax, a ruse. A Horse Camp is definitely something much worse than it was supposed to be. If there's one thing that Percy and I can agree on, it's that Horse Camp is a big, fat joke.

Percy had a short fight with Stretch. It ended up with Percy sleeping outside in the granary, which, instead of punishment, turned out to be a reward in Percy's dumb eyes. He's so immature. He spends tons of time there now. I think he's looking at old football magazines and stuff, though I don't know because I am *not a snoop*. Percy is totally obsessed with football. It's all he talks about, sometimes. I just know that at night, when he's supposed to be saying his prayers, he's actually thinking about football players.

Percy did tell me that when Stretch was yelling at him, he let it slip that he had a son who died. What happened to Stretch's son? Why did he die? Why didn't you tell me? I hope he accepted Jesus as his personal lord and savior before he died. From what I know of Stretch, though, this seems highly unlikely. The apple never falls far from the tree, Dad always says.

Thanks for sending my Zombie Cowboy books to Stretch's farm. I plan to read them very, very carefully so I can develop a good lesson plan for the youth ministry program at Dad's new church. I can't wait to tell all those girls why it's a sin to read about falling in love with zombies or vampires or werewolves. I made a PowerPoint presentation to explain how books in the Zombie Cowboy series use clever, handsome, sweet-talking, 1800s zombie cowboys to romance girls with their southern drawls and good manners. I can't wait to tell all those naïve girls about how reading those books leads to promiscuity. I have a whole ten-minute lecture on how the Zombie Cowboy series encourages the occult and invites the devil into your life. Also, Percy and Pauly each liked the new shoes that you sent, but they probably won't remember to tell you thank you, so I will do it on their behalf.

Thank you. Well, that's about all for now, I guess.

God loves you,

Penny

Dear Dad,

How are the preparations for the new church building going? How exciting! I can't wait to see it. I've got some really good ideas for the youth ministry program that I could be in charge of. I am currently compiling a list of books about vampires, werewolves, zombies, wizards, and witches that no young person should read because, as you have preached many times, those kinds of books invite the occult and the devil into the readers' heart.

You must be very, very busy, since we haven't heard from you in a long time. No worries, though. I'm doing my best to keep the boys and myself out of trouble and in God's grace.

If at all possible, maybe you could arrange to have Percy, Pauly, and me come to the new church's inauguration? I think it's important for us to show the congregation a unified family. Stretch does not attend church, so we haven't attended one service since we've been here.

Please write! I miss you.

Love,

Penelope

Dear Diary,

Yesterday while taking a break from painting these run-down, old bird feeders, a job that Guess Who (yep, Stretch!) gave me, I was snooping around and found a picture of Stretch on his wedding day! Before we came here, I didn't even know Stretch had been married *and* had a son who died, which Mom failed to tell me, so I had to hear it from Percy. He acted like a big know-it-all in the process, of course.

Losing a wife and a son is so sad. These tragedies probably explain why Stretch is so crabby and why he doesn't go to church. He's probably mad at God for taking his family away.

I guess he doesn't know that you have to turn to God, not away from Him, when bad things happen. I've been praying night and day for God to restore my family to the way it was. I just know He can do it if I'm sincere and good enough to deserve it. He can help Mom see how bad she's been and help her change her life for the better. I'm trying to be patient.

Percy is driving me crazy. He never wants to talk about anything important. Like this morning, when I asked him how he was dealing with everything, he said that he was fine. Fine?! I don't think so! I mean, he's living in the middle of nowhere while our parents are getting a divorce! I think he's in denial. Maybe I will try really hard to get him to open up about his true feelings. It's not good to keep them all bundled up the way he is. He acts like everything is just fine, but it's not.

I had a really good talk with Pauly about everything. Since no one else is mature enough to help him through the disintegration of our nuclear family, I guess I have to. I almost wish my conversation with him would have been taped or recorded so Mom could watch it and see how terrible this is for Pauly. If my cell phone had any modern applications, I could have recorded it. But since it doesn't, I couldn't. Luckily, I remember everything.

Firstly, I told Pauly that I knew this was a really hard time for him. I said if he wanted to, he could ask me any questions. He asked me if he could have a Popsicle. I told him that's not the kind of question I meant. Then I told him that he should know that even though Dad and Mom sent us here for a little while, they both still love him a lot, especially Dad.

Pauly was just looking around, not concentrating, a sure sign of distress. I asked him if he was confused about anything. He inquired what the word *lackadaisical* meant, although of course he didn't say it right. When I asked him why, he said it was because Uncle Stretch had commented that Pauly's hair looked like a lackadaisical cat resting on his head. I told Pauly to never mind that, and that his hair looked fine.

Next, I asked Pauly if he was confused about who was in his nuclear family or who is in charge and who he should be listening to. He said that he thought Uncle Stretch was in charge of him, and I told him it was not just Uncle Stretch, but me, too. He asked if Percy was in charge of him, too, but I told him to never mind Percy, which made Pauly smile.

He must have been feeling better then, because he started talking about cartoons, some of which are violent, like SpongeBob SquarePants, but I chalked that up to Pauly's trusting me, and I decided not to shame him for watching cartoons. I just hope he isn't turning to false idols at such an early age!

I asked Pauly if he remembered to pray nightly, and I told him that if he needs guidance or feels lonely, to just talk with God. He said that he forgot to pray two days before, and then he asked me for a Popsicle again. He said Stretch wouldn't give him one because it would give him a tapeworm, which I cannot condone saying to a child. Putting all that fear in his heart is a terrible thing to do unless it's fear of the Lord. I gave him a red Popsicle and a big hug and told him if he wanted to cry on my shoulder, too, he could, but he said he'd rather just eat his Popsicle.

I will have my hands full making sure I'm there for Pauly, so he doesn't crumble under the weight of his feelings of abandonment and confusion.

DEAR OKONKWO,

I ENJOYED RECEIVING THE PHOTOGRAPH OF YOU AND YOUR NEW GOAT. WHAT DO YOU FEED HIM? DOES HE HAVE A NAME? I USED TO LIVE IN AFRICA, TOO, BUT NOW I AM LIVING IN AN AGRICULTURAL COMMUNITY WHERE EVERYONE HELPS EVERYONE, JUST LIKE IN YOUR VILLAGE! I ALSO HAVE MANY CHORES. FOR INSTANCE, I HAVE TO BABYSIT MY BROTHERS, WATER THE HOUSEPLANTS, HANG THE CLOTHES ON THE LINE TO DRY, MAKE SANDWICHES FOR LUNCH, AND FEED THE HORSES AND OTHER ANIMALS. AS YOU CAN SEE, I ALSO HAVE A LOT OF WORK TO DO AND MANY ANIMALS TO CARE FOR, JUST LIKE YOU DO. PROBABLY MORE THAN YOU DO!

WE HAVE SOME COWS, PIGS, CHICKENS, DOGS, AND A COUPLE OF HORSES WHO ARE VERY OLD. WE HAVE MANY, MANY CATS AROUND HERE. DO YOU HAVE A CAT? I AM VERY HAPPY THAT YOU ARE ABLE TO BUY BOOKS FOR SCHOOL WITH THE MONEY I SENT. I HAVE LOTS OF MONEY FOR BOOKS, AND I READ A LOT. YOU WILL SOON BE SURPRISED BY HOW MUCH YOU CAN LEARN FROM A BOOK.

DO YOU HAVE A BIBLE? THAT IS BY FAR THE BEST BOOK THERE IS IN THE WHOLE WORLD. IT IS JUST FULL OF THE GOOD STORIES THAT

TEACH YOU HOW TO LIVE YOUR LIFE. THE BIBLE
TELLS ALL ABOUT JESUS, WHO SAID THE NICEST
THINGS, LIKE THE MEEK SHALL INHERIT THE
EARTH AND BLESSED ARE THE PEACEMAKERS.
THERE ARE SOME OTHER RULES IN THERE, TOO,
LIKE HONOR YOUR FATHER AND MOTHER AND DO
NOT COMMIT ADULTERY OR STEAL OR MURDER
ANYBODY. I READ THAT THERE IS A LOT OF
ADULTERY AND STEALING IN YOUR PART OF THE
WORLD, WHERE NOT EVERYONE KNOWS ABOUT
JESUS YET. MAYBE WHEN YOU GET YOUR BIBLE,
YOU CAN TEACH THE OTHER PEOPLE IN YOUR
LITTLE VILLAGE JESUS'S LESSONS. THAT WOULD
MAKE DONATING ALL THIS MONEY TO YOU
WORTH IT IN MY EYES!

  WRITE SOON,
  PENELOPE PRIBYL

Chapter 5
Percy's Friend Elle

I'VE BEEN SLEEPING out in the granary for a week now, and you know what? I like it. And I like talking to Elle, too. Elle is the finger-sucking woman in the rubber swimsuit with the diving mask on her head and her arm covering one of her breasts, which is bare because it is not covered by the swimsuit for whatever reason, which I don't mind. I know her name is Elle because, on the bottom of the page it says, *Elle's Lisa Lomas suit ($52) should give her an unusual tan.*

The words and the picture are very interesting, but I have major questions. First of all, $52 for a swimsuit? I think my last one cost $9.99, and it does the job. Second of all, that's a lot of money for a swimsuit that only covers one breast. I can't imagine how much it would have cost if it was built for two breasts. Also, she's wearing an expensive-looking watch on her left hand, which is dangling close to the water. But what if the watch isn't water-resistant? I'm certain that watch would've gotten wet the day Elle had her picture taken, and I'm even surer Elle got real ticked if she ruined her watch. Or what if it was borrowed? Maybe she had to make a big apology to whoever's watch it was.

I started talking to Elle the morning after Uncle Stretch put me out of the house. I was just sitting there, wrapped in the old, dusty blanket after I woke up, thinking how one time Dad gave this sermon that wasn't as boring as most of his sermons, so I was listening, and it was about how if you feel alone, you're not, because God's watching you, and He will be your friend. Then I thought, *Hey, as long as God is watching, there might as well be another unreal person or thing watching, so why not a picture hanging on my wall showing a lady in an interesting swimsuit?*

Besides having Elle watch me, I like to watch her. I like the look on her face. I like to wonder what she's thinking. She looks playful, or thoughtful, or just happy. And that swimsuit is really fascinating to think about. Like, why would someone make a swimsuit that only covers part of her top half? If you were actually swimming in it, your one breast would just be out there for everyone to see unless you were constantly remembering to keep your arm there. Also, her right pointer finger is up by her mouth, and she's biting on it like she's shy. Maybe she's nervous—probably about the one-armed suit. Or maybe she's a fingernail biter. I bite mine most of the time, so we have that in common. I think of her as very brave. It was one of the first things I told her. I really feel like she listens to me.

Elle is a big improvement over Pauly and Penny. All Penny does lately is brag about how she's sponsoring this African kid, sending him letters with five bucks—which she guilts Stretch into giving her since she doesn't even have her own money—inside the envelope. The kid probably doesn't even read her letters, just snatches out the five bucks and goes and buys some junk to eat because he's starving. He probably can't even read English. She should just draw him a picture, even though she draws like a kindergartner. Penny acts real nice to people she hasn't even met, which is easy to do until you meet them. You don't see her giving me, her own brother, five dollars. About the only thing she gives me is a headache.

This morning, I stained a hickory fence that pens in Bernie and Brenda. It was a real Horse Camp of a job, since it took about three hours when Uncle Stretch said it would take only one. You try wielding a paintbrush with that mean horse, Brenda, wandering over and trying to bite your hand off about every two minutes! Finally, I got into a groove, painting and dodging Brenda, running back and forth. Bernie just stood there, chewing something, watching me. Man, is he worthless. To think that our parents thought we'd be riding him around this summer! In the end, I think I got most of the fence covered, but I'm sure Uncle Stretch the Perfectionist will find a couple of spots I missed.

With the short remainder of my morning, I have been chucking walnuts, which I have to pretend are footballs since I forgot my real football back in our last home in Rockville, Maryland, which is where we moved after we left the Philippines. What little stuff we had was put into storage. I think there are other storage spaces, too, in different parts of the country, that have our stuff sitting in them. It doesn't bother me, really, other than the football, a couple of jerseys, and this one pair of jeans I had. They'll probably be too small for me by the time I get them back, if I ever do. So I'm aiming the walnuts at this ammonia tank, which I pretend is a wide receiver for the Minnesota Vikings, since it's about half a football field away. When I hit the tank with a walnut, which is hard to do, it sounds like somebody banging a metal drum underwater. It's cool.

After a while, Pauly comes up to me with a stupid red Kool-Aid stain around his mouth, and I say to him, "Hey, dork, nice Kool-Aid stain around your mouth."

"Shut up, P.P.," says Pauly.

"Just because Uncle Stretch is gone this morning doesn't mean you can drink all the Kool-Aid, Pauly," I say.

"I didn't!" says Pauly. "Just a couple of dwinks is all I had."

"Whatever," I say. "You want to play catch or something?"

"Shoh."

"Go over by the ammonia tank, then."

"Whey-oh is that?"

"By that white tank, stupid," I say, pointing.

"What tank?"

"That thing that looks like a big, white hot dog, see?" I point. "Over there where all those stinky green and brown walnuts are lying on the ground?"

"I see it," says Pauly, "but why ow you thwowing walnuts at an aminal tank?"

"The reason I'm throwing walnuts at the *ammonia* tank is that I'm pretending the tank is a wide receiver for the Vikings."

"Oh," says Pauly, and runs off. He runs funny, like, his knees go way up. I don't know if they run different where he came from or what, but it just looks ridiculous to me. He looks like he's in a fast-motion marching band or something. The only thing he's missing is a miniature tuba.

"Here you go, moron," I say, and chuck one hard at him. He doesn't realize I'm throwing at him rather than to him, and the walnut whizzes by his ear before he gets a chance to try to catch it. He runs after it, picks it up, and cocks his arm to throw it back.

"No, no, you dope," I say, "you don't have to throw it back," but Pauly's throw is already in the air, and it lands way short—about halfway between us. He runs after it again, picks it, up and fires. This time, the walnut goes straight out to the side, looping in a dumb arc. He runs after it again.

"Pauly!" I yell. "Leave it be! I got a whole pile here, so you don't have to throw them back. Just try to catch."

He looks at me like I'm the foreigner, then what I've said sinks into his brain—I can see it on his face. I bet most kids his age are much smarter than he is. He'll probably flunk out of kindergarten next year. He runs back to his original spot by the ammonia tank.

"This one's for the Vikings wide receiver," I say, and lob one really high, though I'm still aiming for Pauly's head. He runs in a pattern that makes it look like he's trying to draw a star with his feet, and he lunges at it before the walnut thuds just a couple of feet in front of him into the grass.

"You're supposed to stand still," I say. "That one was for the Vikings guy, not you!"

"But why thwow it to the Vikings guy?" says Pauly. "He can't catch."

"You must be legally dumb," I say. "Now just hold still when it's the Vikings guy's turn or you're out of the game, Pauly!" I yell. He just looks at me with his eyebrows—which are really bushy for a kid's—scrunched down and his chin pointed into his chest. It's his mad look. "Get ready now," I say, " 'cause this one's for you." I whip it at him, and it misses his head by inches. He reacts a second late again, swatting at it like it's a fly.

"All right, now this one's for the Vikings guy," I say, and throw one high. It lands next to Pauly's side, but he doesn't move. Perfect. My target is secure.

"This one's yours," I say, and fire. Way off. "You gotta dive for those," I say. Pauly nods his head.

"Vikings guy's," I say. It looks to be right on target, but Pauly ducks out of the way at the last second. It would've hit him for sure, maybe even knocked him over, which would've been really funny, even if I got in trouble for it. "You're supposed to stand still!" I bellow. "The Vikings guy will catch those."

He looks confused, because he knows the ammonia tank isn't a Vikings wide receiver who can catch walnuts, but he just says, "Soh-wee," and puts his little hands up to show he's ready for his turn.

After a while, Pauly kind of figures out that I'm trying to nail him with walnuts, so it isn't that fun anymore, and I tell him that I will be moving on to some cardio training.

"What's cow-dio twaining?"

"You're too young for it," I say. "So go find something else to do."

"Okay," he says, and runs off. It's like he doesn't even get it sometimes when I'm slamming him.

I do five sets of forty-yard sprints across the farmyard. Then I decide to go on a longer run. If I want to be the best, I have to put in the work. At the end of the driveway, just before I have to decide to go left or right, up comes Uncle Stretch's pickup with a big trailer hitched to the back end. He turns in the driveway, and I stop running, suddenly feeling guilty about trying to hit Pauly in the head with those walnuts.

"What you running from?" says Uncle Stretch, hanging his head out the window.

"Oh, just training for football," I say. "I was doing some cardio because if I want to be the best, I—" I realize there's another person in the cab of the truck. Two other persons. One old, one young. Both femaliens.

"Percy, meet Sheryl and Sherylynn."

"Which is which?" I say.

Uncle Stretch glares at me.

"I'm Sheryl," says the older woman, reaching across Uncle Stretch to shake my hand. I reach up to grab her hand, but when I do, I notice I can see right down Sheryl's shirt. Her bra is purple. Yii! I look away.

"You can call me June Bug," says the younger one, smiling. She looks about my age.

"Hi," I say. I don't smile back.

"You finish staining that hickory fence like I told you?" Uncle Stretch asks.

"Oh, shoot," I say. "Forgot."

Uncle Stretch looks at Sheryl like, *Oh, see what I have to put up with, with this kid around this summer?*

"Just kidding!" I say. "I finished that an hour ago." I show him my stained hands as proof.

Uncle Stretch squints at me like he's trying to think of a way I might be lying to him.

Sheryl says, "Just tell him about the chickens!"

Uncle Stretch looks over his shoulder toward the big trailer. "See that horse trailer? There's a bunch of chickens in there. You can use a couple of them, so you have something to show at the county fair coming up next month."

"You mean we're still gonna be here next month?" I say.

Sheryl and Uncle Stretch look at each other. "Looks like," says Uncle Stretch.

"I thought you already had chickens," I say to Uncle Stretch.

"I do, but you'll find the birds in this trailer a little more, say, *qualified* for fair competition."

"Sounds boring to me."

Uncle Stretch gives me the *You better be respectful, buddy* look.

Sheryl smiles at me and says, "You ever been to a county fair?"

"Of course," I say, even though I haven't.

"Well," says Sheryl, "June Bug's gonna show you and your little brother how to clean these chickens up real nice and help you practice showing them. She's twelve, just like you."

"Fabulous," I say.

Sheryl looks past my head at Pauly jogging up the driveway. "So that's the little one?" she says to Uncle Stretch. "Oh, is he ever cute!"

"He's adopted," I say. Uncle Stretch frowns and opens his mouth to say something, but I cut him off by saying, "Well, I better get back to my workout now. See ya!" I begin jogging away.

"You'll need to sweep out that grain bin before supper," says Uncle Stretch.

"Whatever," I say over my shoulder.

I sprint away from the truck. I feel like running for miles.

Chapter 6

PENNY PONDERS TEMPTATION

Dear Diary,

I knew it! The big-breasted, flirty beautician from the beauty parlor and her daughter came by the farm today, hitching a ride in Stretch's old jalopy of a pickup truck, which was pulling a big horse trailer with a bumper sticker that said, I Love Horses! I was hoping and praying that Stretch had finally come to his senses and decided to ship out Brenda, that nasty old horse of his, who seems to take great joy in lifting her rubbery lips and snorting and biting! Every time I go near her, she shows her big teeth and stamps her hooves like she can't wait to charge after me and kill me. Stretch thinks her poor disposition is no big deal. Here's an example of a previous conversation between us on the subject of Brenda:

Me: (My voice calm and very polite.) Stretch, your horse is going to kill somebody.

Stretch: (Rude voiced and acting like there's a simple explanation for everything.) Stay away from her, then.

Me: I'm pretty sure that horse may need some medical attention or maybe needs to be sold. She's very violent and angry.

Stretch: (Walking away, practically ignoring me.) Mind your own business, Penny.

Anyway, looks like that Brenda is here to stay, even though it's very obvious that she has some kind of personality disorder. She was probably abused when she was a filly. At the least she was talked to very rudely, like the way Stretch talks to me, which can lead to serious problems later in life.

This lady Sheryl might be Stretch's girlfriend. I'm usually very perceptive about things like this. Sheryl has a daughter, named Sherylynn, whom everybody calls June Bug, and who treats Stretch like he's her dad or something. She jumps on him and tackles him very playfully even though she's my age, twelve, and shouldn't be acting like that anymore. That's more like how Pauly should act. Stretch doesn't seem to mind, though, and he picks her up and acts like he's going to throw her in the horse's water tank or in the back of the truck, but he doesn't. I've never seen a grown man act so childish before. I think it really bothers Sheryl because she shakes her head and puts her hands on her hips and asks what she is going to do with the two of them. Anyway, I think June Bug (what an immature nickname) has got the hots for Percy. She spent all afternoon laughing and acting happy to meet the boys and saying things like, *This is great!* and holding Pauly's hand like he's *her* little brother and not mine. Then she helped Percy and Pauly clean out the chicken coop because, get this, the boys are now the proud parents of about three million dirty chickens that they're going to show at the county fair! They asked me if I wanted to show one, too, but I don't even have to tell you my answer.

June Bug is not very attractive, if you ask me, but I didn't say that to her. When I met her, I was polite and acted very mature because that's how Dad taught me to act when I meet new people so that I can set an example for them.

June Bug: (Wearing yellow shorts and a yellow top, as if that really looks nice, and then having the audacity to give me a big, giant hug, as if we're family or something.) You must be Penny! I'm really happy to meet you!

Me: (Wearing a very modest T-shirt from a Bible

camp that Dad once ran and some jean shorts that go almost to my knees.) It's a pleasure to meet you, too, Sherylynn.

June Bug: Oh, you can call me June Bug. Everyone does. I know it's a little dumb, but I'm used to it.

Me: My Christian name is Penelope Rachel. But everyone calls me Penny.

June Bug: My best friend at school's name is Rachel. I love that name. You'll really like her, too, if you ever get to meet her.

Me: We won't be here long enough for me to meet her. Rachel was the name of the beautiful wife of Jacob. He had to work fourteen years to earn the right to marry her.

June Bug: Wow! Are they your relatives or something? I mean, how do you know Jacob and Rachel?

Me: Jacob from the Bible? Have you heard of the Bible?

June Bug: Oh. Yeah, I know about the Bible a little. Not as much as you, though.

Me: Jacob was the son of Isaac, who was almost sacrificed by his father, Abraham, before God intervened in all His mercy and saved him.

June Bug: I didn't know that. Rachel must have been really beautiful for Jacob to work all those years.

Me: Well, he thought he only had to work seven

years for her, but her dad tricked Jacob into marrying her older sister, Leah, who wasn't nearly as attractive as Rachel, and then made him work another seven years to get to have Rachel, too.

June Bug: What?! That's wild! That Bible sounds like the soap operas my mom watches.

Me: No, it isn't like a soap opera at all, but you should really read it for yourself.

Anyway, June Bug just said one dumb thing after another. I couldn't believe she had never even heard of Rachel from the Bible! Even the dumbest kid knows about her. And even though she asked me if I wanted to help with the chickens, I could tell she really hoped I'd say no, which I did, so she could have Percy and Pauly all to herself.

Later, Stretch and Sheryl went on a horse ride together on Brenda (even sitting in the same saddle!) and didn't come back for a long, long time. They were gone long enough to do some sinful things for sure. Sheryl was only wearing a thin tank top that was sure to lure Stretch's eyes to her bosom. *And* she was wearing jeans with a hole in the butt cheek, and I saw skin underneath, so that means she either A) was wearing a thong, or B) wasn't wearing any underwear at all. Either way, *temptation city.*

I would have followed them, but I couldn't because,

for once, Stretch wouldn't let Pauly come with him, so I had to babysit. As soon as Stretch said, "Pauly, you stay here with Penny," I *knew* something was up. I mean, Pauly sits right outside the bathroom door while Stretch goes to the bathroom, even when the stench coming from inside is enough to make anyone, human or animal, pass out. That's probably what happened to Stretch's family. He probably stunk them to death.

Seriously, not knowing what happened to his family is driving me crazy! I mean, it could be anything. He could be divorced. Or, his wife could have died, like his son. Or maybe he could have her hidden in the attic like that guy in *Jane Eyre*! I mean, how am I supposed to live here without knowing whether or not I'm in the same house as a psychotic killer! One of these days, I'm going to snoop in every box and trunk until I get to the bottom of what's going on around here.

Dear Mom,

I am *not* being nosy. Wanting to know what happened to Stretch's family is a natural thing. What is the big secret? If I were you, I'd be very worried that I'd be endangering my everlasting soul by covering up the crime of my brother. The Lord's work is supposed to be your first priority, not being an accomplice to Stretch's crime! But, then again, what do *you* care about crime? Apparently, the laws of God and the laws of the United States simply don't apply to *you*. *You*, apparently, can feel free to do whatever *you* want.

And, as far as Stretch's relationship with Sheryl goes, it *is* my business because I'm not comfortable with two unmarried people having sexual relations around my brothers, which I know Stretch and Sheryl are doing. And, no, I don't think that what happens between two consenting adults is fine and dandy and none of my business. I'd think that, as our mother, you would be concerned about the type of example Stretch is setting for us and would be writing to Daddy to tell him to come and pick us up and bring us home. While you're at it, you can tell Daddy you're sorry, so we can just put all this ridiculous business behind us. But, apparently, the rules of motherhood don't apply to *you*, either. If you didn't want to raise us, why did you even have us?! Why have kids at all if you're just going to abandon them?! Sometimes I wish I was never even born!!!

(I had to take a break to calm down, but now I am back.)

Thanks for sending the information on breast development. I knew all of the information already, but I can't help wondering why mine don't grow. I've read that breast size is genetic, so I was just wondering why mine didn't look more like yours yet. You know, really full and round. It may be due to low estrogen or a problem with my pituitary gland.

Remember all those African girls whose mothers would start ironing and pounding down their breasts at ages nine and ten? Weird! If my daughter started developing breasts early, I would never do that. I would tell her that she looks beautiful, and she's lucky! Remember when you held a medical seminar to tell the mothers about the pain and damage they were inflicting upon their daughters, and they just looked at you like *you* were the weird one? Like you didn't understand that their daughters were under constant sexual pressure from the men in their village. Like you didn't understand that they wanted educations for their daughters rather than early marriages and babies. Like you didn't get that they really believed that stalling breast development could improve their daughters' lives. C'mon, ladies! I studied those girls really hard, and it was clear that breast ironing did not stop their development in the least. You can't stop progress and shouldn't mess with nature. Someone should have told those mothers that.

Yes, I am enjoying my books, but only because I'm finding so many things about them that are sinful. I will have no problem developing an entire curriculum about the need to censor all zombie, werewolf, and vampire books. In *Zombie Cowboy*, the main character, Eamon Cloversniffer, falls in love with the beautiful and thoughtful and very poor Patience Lonelyheart, who has to take care of her dying father before she marries the town's richest man, who is the mean and terrible Handle Boomton. Patience, who has long and glorious hair just like mine, admires Eamon's pale skin and red lips and tender voice and especially the way he calls her Honey Dear, but then he admits to her that he is a zombie and is doomed to walk the earth for eternity. Eamon Cloversniffer loves Patience so much but can't marry her or he will destine her to the same terrible fate. But, now Patience and Eamon are debating whether they should turn Patience's father into a zombie so that he never dies, and she'll never have to marry Handle Boomton. I must say, the book is very interesting. I can see why so many young girls read these books and get swept away and on the road to hell before they even know what happened. Lucky for me, I know that what I am reading is pure sinful temptation.

Have you heard from Daddy? He sent an envelope with money to Stretch with a Post-it note that said, *For school clothing and supplies*. Why is Stretch supposed to take us school shopping? Daddy said we'd be home long before school started.

And what do you mean that I should "prepare

myself for the worst" regarding your chances for an acquittal? Seriously, Mom. You can't honestly be thinking of going to prison over all this nonsense! Daddy told you he'd testify on your behalf if you'd just publicly say you're sorry and repent. Wouldn't it be exciting if Daddy brought you to the front of the new church and laid his hands on you in cleansing and forgiveness and did that thing in which he calls down the power of the Spirit and all the people shout and lift their hands and pray to the Lord? Maybe you could even tremble and cry and fall to your knees, and all the congregation could call out, *Heal her, Jesus. Heal her, Jesus*. And Daddy would finally banish the devil from your body and then lift you to your feet and kiss your forehead and say, *You are forgiven, Sister. You are healed. Go and sin no more*. Wouldn't that be great?! Remember how Daddy would get so moved by the Spirit working in him that his forehead would get real sweaty and his hair would stick to his face? Mother, please call him and say you're sorry! Please. Please. Please. I don't think you understand how important this is to me.

    Love,
    Penny

Dear Daddy,
    I haven't heard from you in a while. I know you are

very busy with the new church building.

I believe Mom is ready to ask you for forgiveness. I think she's realized that she caused the disintegration of our nuclear family and wants to put it back together. I think that if you called or visited her, we could put all this behind us. Timing is very important. The devil is here on our uncle's farm. I am sure of it. Some sinful things are happening that require your immediate attention. I pray really hard to keep the evil at bay, but I am only twelve and am not sure that I have your strength as a holy person.

Blessings in Jesus's name,

Penelope

Chapter 7
PERCY AND JUNE BUG

JUNE BUG used to bug me, but she doesn't as much anymore. I thought early on she had a crush on me, which would've been annoying and something I've had to deal with before. When I was in foreign lands and the only white boy running around, I think girls just liked me because I looked different. *Exotic*, or whatever the word is. Now that I've been around June Bug for a couple of weeks, training chickens together, I can see she's more into the chickens than boys, at this point. Fine by me! We've got some serious work to do before we show them at the fair.

"You gotta wash 'em three days before the show so you get 'em clean but they still have enough time to get their natural oils back," says June Bug, looking over the flock.

Pauly's over in the corner of the henhouse, running at the chickens and then skidding to a stop, which makes them start clucking and flapping around. "Hey," I yell. "Knock it off, Pauly! We don't want them flapping their wings or spazzing out at the judges."

Pauly does it again and almost steps on Carl, an old banty rooster who's too slow to get out of the way.

"Pauly!" I shout. "Leave Carl alone!"

June Bug grabs my arm. "It's okay, Pers. He's just a kid."

"He's an idiot!" I say.

"Ah, just leave him be," she says. She pats me on the back and smiles. Before I know it, I smile back. Like I said in the beginning, June Bug seemed bossy, a lot like her mom or Penny, but lately, she's been pretty cool. She's about the only one around here who doesn't yell at me, and she is fun to play with. Like play catch, you know, or play tag, or work, or whatever. Not like play "house" or anything.

"Today we need to pick the ones we're gonna show and check 'em for diseases and stuff before we wash 'em," June Bug says. "You want to pick first?"

"Nah, you go first," I say.

June Bug shrugs and walks over to a group of ten or

twelve chickens all pecking at the ground. Pauly's got Carl cornered and is shuffling his feet at him. Nobody wants to show Carl, anyway. He looks like some of the straggly chickens we used to see in Africa or the Philippines. That's probably why Pauly likes messing with Carl—reminds him of home.

June Bug bends down and gently gathers one of the bigger chickens into her arms, cradling it like a running back who just took a handoff. The chicken clucks once and is quiet. She brings it over to the table where we'll do our washing business.

"Looks pretty good," I say.

"He's all right," says June Bug. "I left the tamest, best-looking ones for you and Pauly. I've done this before, and half of showing is just letting your birds know you're calm, and being confident about your overall chicken knowledge when the judge asks you questions."

She looks her chicken over, stretching his wings out and combing through his feathers with her fingers. It barely makes a sound. It looks like it might even be enjoying June Bug touching it. Then June Bug stares, close up, at its feet.

"What are you doing that for?" I say.

"Checking for bumblefoot, or other diseases you can see with the naked eye."

I blush at that. *Naked*. Suddenly, Pauly's right next

to us, asking questions. "You mean the chickens get sick?" he says.

"Of course they do, stupid," I say, elbowing him out of the way.

"Do they bawf oh have a cough?" asks Pauly.

"Pauly, you're a real dummy," I say.

"No, you're not, Pauly," says June Bug. She takes a long strand of hair that came loose from her ponytail and tucks it back behind her ear. "I've seen lots of chickens with diseases."

"How many?" says Pauly.

"Well, once we had to kill our entire flock—pullorum took hold, and by law you have to get rid of any chicken with pullorum."

"Jeez," I say. I wonder if pullorum is like leprosy or what. People in the Bible were always getting that and then having to go off by themselves.

"No," says Pauly. "I meant how many diseases?"

"I don't know, dude," she says. "Lots. There's quite a few."

"What ahw they called?"

"Shut up, Pauly!" I say. "You wouldn't even understand!"

"Well," says June Bug, "there's bumblefoot, fowl pox, rot gut, swollen head syndrome, gray eye, parrot fever, helicopter disease. . . ."

"Whoa," says Pauly.

"Different strains of egg drop syndrome are some of the most common," she says. "When your hens lay less and less eggs, you know something's up."

"I think Cah-wel might have egg dwop syndwome," says Pauly.

"Roosters can't lay eggs, you dipstick!" I shout.

"He's just old, that's why he looks so gaunt," says June Bug. "My mom says he used to be the king of Stretch's flock, though. Like probably back in the days when Stretch's son was still alive."

"Roland?" I say. "You know about Roland?"

"Naw, not really," June Bug says. She scratches behind her chicken's head. I swear, the chicken smiles. "Just that I guess Stretch changed a lot when he died—that's what my mom says, anyways. He used to be wilder, I think. Grab yours now, Pers," she says.

"Nah," I say, "let Pauly go next."

"You're afraid to hold 'em, still?"

"No!"

"Well, pick one up, then."

I start windmilling my arms and holding my foot behind my back to stretch my quads.

"What are you doing?" asks June Bug.

"Stretching, obviously," I say.

"You're just wasting time," says June Bug. "You must have some issues with being afraid of live animals."

"He's always been pwetty scay-ohd of animals," says Pauly.

"At least I'm an American citizen!" I say.

June Bug glares at me. "Anyway, if you're done stretching now, it's your turn," she says, "unless you're too scared."

"I'm not scared of anything," I say. I walk over to where most of the chickens stand around, pecking at the dirt or just looking bored. I take a good look, moving slowly so they don't start squawking or jutting their freaky necks or flapping their dusty wings. I look back at June Bug and Pauly, and I see Penny sticking her head in the barn door, spying.

"What are you doing here?" I yell.

Penny's head disappears, and you can hear her running away, her shoes mashing gravel. Shaking my head, I turn back to the chickens and find one that looks fat and slow. I crack a couple of knuckles and stretch my neck by bobbing my head side to side. This is the part I hate. I can just picture it flapping and clawing at me, drawing blood or worse. I get low and quickly jolt my hands around its body, and the thing practically screams at me, beating its wings in my face. I jump back and look over to June Bug. "Dang!" I say.

Pauly looks up at June Bug and says, "He's scay-ohd."

"Put a sock in it, dunderhead!" I yell at Pauly.

"Just stay calm," says June Bug. "Imagine your arms are cotton balls."

"Um, these things have way too many muscles in them for that to happen," I say. I flex.

June Bug shakes her head. "How long you think this'll take?" she says.

After two more tries, I nab one, and June Bug has her answer.

At the dinner table, Sheryl stands over me, dishing up some mashed potatoes. Apparently, she and June Bug are now being invited to family dinners in Stretch's dining room. I can tell it bugs Penny because she can barely look at Sheryl or June Bug without rolling her eyes. Sheryl bends way over me, and I can see her bra again—jeez! It's light blue today. Then Uncle Stretch comes in with the main course on a big plate and sets it down.

"Chicken?" I say. "You've got to be kidding!"

He gives me the evil eye, starts to say something, then looks at Sheryl, who shows him this little smile. This chain reaction has been happening a lot lately. Uncle Stretch takes a deep breath. He picks up a knife, hacks off a leg, thunks it down on my plate, and says, "Yep. Chicken."

"I don't think I can do this," I say. "No disrespect, Uncle Stretch, but I've been working with these things all day, and it just doesn't seem right."

Sheryl takes a seat, and Uncle Stretch goes on hacking up the chicken, not saying anything but slinging pieces on everybody's plate, one by one. June Bug tears right in, as if we hadn't just spent the entire afternoon washing our own chickens.

I look at Penny, and she looks at Uncle Stretch. The only time she sides with me anymore is when I'm against Uncle Stretch, which is pretty common. But still, it's more about her rebelling against Uncle Stretch than supporting me. Pauly follows June Bug's example, chewing loudly as he wolfs down the meat.

"How can you two eat that?" I say.

"Perseus," says Uncle Stretch. Sheryl puts her hand on Uncle Stretch's arm.

"But," I say, "what if that thing had parrot fever or rot gut?"

Everybody looks at me like I'm crazy—except Penny, who seems suddenly very interested. "What's parrot fever?" she says.

"It's rare," says June Bug. "Beak discharge, conjunctivitis, diarrhea, green feces."

"What's rot gut?" asks Penny.

"A bacteria," says June Bug. "It causes the bird's feces to smell, well, worse than normal or look slightly darker because of blood staining, and the bird may become emaciated. Highly treatable, though."

"Hey, I've heard of that," says Penny. "I've heard of the avian flu, too. This chicken could very well have that."

"Doubtful," says June Bug.

"It might have egg dwop sydwome, too," says Pauly.

"He's right," I say. "Lots of chickens get egg drop syndrome—ask June Bug. I'll just give mine to Penny. She doesn't mind eating diseased chickens." I pick up my plate and shove it in her direction. "Here you go, Penny."

Penny screeches and jumps back from the table. "I'm not eating this chicken," she says. "It definitely could be contaminated. I've seen that barn, and it's not very clean. Who knows what the living conditions were even like for this chicken?"

Uncle Stretch bangs his fist down on the table and the silverware rings. "That does it!" he says. He gets up from the table and storms into the kitchen and out through the screen door with a slam.

We all look at Sheryl, the only adult left. She smiles at June Bug. "Did you tell these kids about all the chicken diseases you've researched?"

"Not all of them," says June Bug.

"They-oh's quite a few," says Pauly, taking a bite of drumstick.

"Kids," says Sheryl. "This chicken is perfectly healthy to eat. However, if you don't want to eat chicken tonight, just have some mashed potatoes, corn, and salad." She takes a deep breath and lets it out, like she's real overwhelmed.

"Jeez, why's everybody gotta get so bent out of shape?" I say.

"We're just following the leader, the guy who had an aneurysm and walked away from the dinner table," says Penny. "The guy who's *always* having an aneurysm."

Sheryl stares at Penny with a sad look, but Penny just takes a big spoonful of corn, dumps it on her mashed potatoes, mixes it around, and shovels a big bite into her mouth. Sometimes she can be worse than me when it comes to disrespect.

Chapter 8
PENNY HAS QUESTIONS

Dear Diary,

Knowing right and wrong was so, so much easier when we lived together with Mom and Dad, when we worshipped together and Daddy taught us the path to heaven. The recent dinner table argument last night has gotten me thinking how topsy-turvy things are now. It's nearly midnight, but I can't sleep. Stretch called us all together tonight to watch the ten o'clock news even though that's usually when we're forced to go to bed. Right away, I knew something was up because he normally doesn't let anyone watch TV. Sheryl and June Bug were there, too. Sheryl looked sympathetic (even though she was wearing a really inappropriate sundress) and bustled around getting glasses of water for everyone and putting boxes of Kleenex here and there as though we were getting ready for a funeral, which, it turns out, we sort of were.

Stretch sat down and patted his knee, and Pauly climbed right up and snuggled in close to the crook of Stretch's neck. Then the news came on, and Stretch told us to be quiet. The very first story was about Mom. Mom's been in the newspaper lots of times but this was the first time her case was on TV. How embarrassing! I always thought that if I were on TV, I would be sitting with an orphan or poor kid from a foreign country, asking for donations to build schools and houses and wells. It turns out I'm the daughter of a criminal! An anchor lady outside the courthouse pointed back to the big, brick building where Mom's future was being decided.

The news story included hand-drawn pictures of a woman who looked like Mom but was way thinner. The drawing showed her sitting at a table with a lawyer guy who didn't look very competent, in my opinion. He was pretty fat and wore tiny glasses. Mom wore a suit jacket, which looked really nice in a hand-drawn kind of way, so at least she didn't embarrass me the way Sheryl would if she were my mother and had to go to court and be on TV in the trampy outfits she wears. If Sheryl had to go to court and someone had to draw a picture of her, they'd probably draw fig leaves to cover up all of her private parts that are always halfway sticking out of her clothes.

As soon as I saw that drawing of Mom, it felt like a raw potato got stuck in my throat. I took a strand of my hair and put it in my mouth, just to have something to bite on. Mom makes me really mad, but she's still my mother, even if she did embarrass me and ruin our family and almost ruin Dad's church. Even though sometimes I have to admit that Mom did have a couple of valid points regarding Dad's ministry, which confuses me, because Dad is the head of the household and head of our nuclear family, so he is always supposed to be right. But when I think about it, I suppose asking all those poor people for more and more money doesn't seem all the way correct. And emailing and calling all those old people, asking for checks probably isn't an all-the-way right thing to do, either.

I mean, if Mom really didn't believe in what Dad was doing and really didn't think his motives were pure in collecting money from all the donors and stuff, there were probably a million other ways to deal with it rather than getting arrested for giving out medical aid for free and being on the evening news. Even though I think about our family's situation almost constantly, I still can't understand it or figure out how to fix it.

Sometimes, I sort of feel like Anne Frank, a girl killed by the Nazis, who wrote a really good book called *Anne Frank: The Diary of a Young Girl*. In it, she talks about being "a bundle of contradictions." I feel *exactly* like that, too. Many times, I wish I had someone smart like her to talk to. And even though Anne Frank never accepted Jesus Christ as her personal Lord and Savior, I think she's in heaven, and I'll probably get to meet her someday, and I have a feeling we'll really hit it off way better than I hit it off with June Bug, who doesn't know much about pain and suffering.

I looked around to see how Percy and Pauly were reacting to seeing Mom on TV, but the room was dim, and I couldn't tell if they had tears in their eyes or not. I did, but I didn't want anyone to see. I miss Mom so much, but I didn't want people to think that I feel sorry for her or for myself because of what she brought on herself, Dad, and all of us. Sometimes, you just have to let people suffer for their own sins, or they will never learn their lesson. Sometimes, you have to cut your losses, like Dad always says.

Then the news anchor said that the verdict was guilty and the sentence was five to seven years in prison. My whole body started to sweat, but I felt really cold, which is exactly how I felt when I got malaria that one time and Mom took care of me day and night. Percy yelled, "What?" And then he yelled, "No. No way!" Another picture of Mom standing to hear the verdict flashed on the screen.

And then Stretch, who hardly ever says anything nice about anyone, said, "You kids look hard at that woman. There goes one of the last martyrs for a truly good cause."

And even though I don't understand exactly what that means, I think it's quite a compliment. The camera panned to a bunch of people with signs and candles lit for Mom! A reporter interviewed one of the supporters, an older, smart-looking woman who said, "They've put the wrong person on trial, and I'm ashamed to live in a country where a good woman like this goes to prison for doing what's right." One person held up a sign that said, PUT THE PHARMACEUTICAL COMPANIES ON TRIAL! Another sign said, WOMEN'S HEALTH CARE IS THE WHOLE WORLD'S PROBLEM!

Those people made me remember Anne Frank again, and how, if you really think about it, Anne Frank and her family were breaking the law by not going to ghettos like the Nazis wanted them to. It made me think that sometimes laws are wrong.

But then I thought, that can't be right, because what if everyone thought they were above the law? If you ask me, it's really hard to figure out when you should follow the law or when you should break it, like Anne Frank and Mom.

Sheryl brought a Kleenex to Percy, and even though he's twelve years old, like me, he bawled like a baby into her chest. He was crying so hard I don't even think he thought one second about Sheryl's enormous breasts in an inappropriate way. Pauly is too little to understand. He asked Stretch if Mom was coming to live at the farm now, too. And Stretch told him not just yet. Pauly said that when she did come, she could share his room.

Stretch said for us not to worry too much because they would appeal the ruling. He said that it was important for us kids to see our mom and see how much support was out there for her.

I have to admit that all those signs and protestors surprised me. I didn't know that anyone was actually on Mom's side. I mean, for crying out loud, she committed some real crimes. And you can't just run around breaking laws whenever you want to. But when I said that, Stretch said that when the laws hurt the common folks, someone needs to break them. That sort of sounds right, too, but it's not what Dad says at all. Not even close.

Dad believes in following the laws and rules. And I, for one, was much happier when we were all just following the laws as a family. Then Pauly said he was going to beat up all those cops handcuffing Mom and break her out of jail, and I had to go to my room because I couldn't take any more and was close to crying.

I'm not one for being dramatic or crying or getting hysterical in public, but what Pauly said nearly did me in, so I just lay on my bed, staring up at the ceiling. After a little while, June Bug came knocking and asked if I was all right.

It really bugged me that she was being so nosy and acting like she was my friend when we're not even related and don't even know each other. I told her I was fine. She told me not to worry and that I'd be stronger for all of these trials. I was about to get really mad at her for talking to me like she was the adult and I was the kid when she told me this:

June Bug: You know, my dad's in prison, too.
Me: (My mouth goes dry, and I swallow. June Bug doesn't look like the type of person who knows someone in prison. Granted, she looks a little *more* like a person who knows someone in prison than I do. But still, I am surprised.)
June Bug: I think you should be proud of your mom. She's going to prison for a good cause. She was helping sick people who couldn't afford medicine and making sure big companies didn't use poor people as

lab rats. It's actually noble. I wish I could say that about my dad.

Me: But what she was doing was illegal! (Sometimes I am amazed at how quickly my emotions can change from sadness to anger. It feels easier to be mad than sad, and I am starting to get really mad at June Bug for being such a know-it-all. First chicken diseases and now prison.)

June Bug: I think it's relative. Some good deeds are illegal. That doesn't mean they're wrong, though. At least, I don't think so.

Me: (That sounds exactly like something Mom would say. Somehow, though, it sounds different from a person my age, even if it is June Bug. I've never even heard a person my age use the word *relative* like that before.) Why's your dad in jail?

June Bug: Something bad. He had a meth lab in his barn.

Me: (Trying not to look surprised so I can avoid hurting her feelings, even though making illegal drugs is really, really bad.) You must be so mad at him.

June Bug: I used to be. But I'm not anymore. Now I'm actually kind of proud of him. He's been in prison for three years already. He's gotten his GED in there and is even taking college courses. He wants to work at a rehab center when he gets out.

Me: Do you think your mom and dad will get back together then?

June Bug: No, because they were never really together in the first place and just conceived me on a fling. Mom said they went to a concert, met in the mosh pit, got matching tattoos, and conceived me all on the same night. But Dad had a different girlfriend already and wasn't looking for a new one.

Me: (Not too surprised after I consider the way Sheryl dresses.) I'm sorry about that.

June Bug: (Shrugs.) It's okay. I'm actually pretty okay with it. People do wild and crazy things sometimes, but that doesn't mean they're bad people or bad parents. I really like and love both my parents. I even really like my dad's girlfriend, Harmony. And I love Stretch, too.

Me: (I think about how many of Stretch's qualities I don't like and try to figure out which of Stretch's qualities June Bug loves.) Wow, June Bug. You are one understanding person.

June Bug: Well, if you're not understanding about people's faults, pretty soon you won't have any people in your life, because all people have them.

Me: Not my dad. He doesn't. That's why he's a minister.

June Bug: (Just smiles at me.)

Me: Thanks, June Bug. G'night.

June Bug: G'night, Penny.

Then she left my room and closed the door softly. At first, I was pretty mad that she acted like she was more understanding than me, but then I decided that judging her for bragging was not practicing understanding on my part, so I just forgave her for bragging. Then I thought about how weird it was that June Bug had given me advice when *I* am the minister's daughter, when *I* am the one who should be in the moral position to give advice, and she's just the daughter of a druggy and a promiscuous woman. And she's giving me advice?! I always imagine myself to be the person keeping it all together, the person with the answers, the person *other* people come to for advice.

Though I wasn't surprised that it's true, I *was* surprised to hear June Bug admit to being randomly conceived by her parents. She practically bragged about being illegitimate and not coming from a nuclear family. I don't think she knows that the disintegration of the nuclear family is at the heart of all the world's troubles and sins.

I've been wondering about Dad. Where is he? Why doesn't he write more often? I know he has a lot of work to do, getting the new church up and running, but I've been wondering if he's choosing God over Percy, Pauly, and me? I know you're supposed to put God first in your life, but you should also find time for your family and especially your own children. I know

Mom chose her illegal crimes over her family. Dad said it a hundred times before we had to come here. Dad said she knew the consequences and did it, anyway. But now it kind of feels like he's choosing his church over us, too.

I feel like both my parents have chosen other things over their own kids. I mean, Sheryl's not what I would call a wonderful role model or appropriate dresser, but at least she's taking care of June Bug and hugs her and kisses her as though June Bug is the greatest kid in the world. And Sheryl's also really, really nice to Percy and Pauly, as if she thinks of them as her own kids. She makes them dinner and tells them to comb their hair. I even saw her lick her finger and then wipe a dirt smudge off Percy's chin. She's not related to us in any way and has absolutely no obligation to be nice to us. But she is. Things are just really, really out of whack around here.

Dear Mom,

Thanks for the letter. I miss you, and I love you, too.

I'm glad to hear that there's a chance for an appeal. I heard Stretch and Sheryl talking the other night about a second mortgage to pay for a better lawyer. That guy you had looked not very professional, in my opinion. The other side's lawyers looked wayyyyy better. They had much nicer suits and more expensive watches. Also, they kept their pens in their pockets, which looks really professional and serious. Maybe you should get a guy like that, a guy who looks like he has it all together. Judges respect that.

I hear you're trying to get a trial by jury. Maybe you could get some of those people who were outside the courtroom when the verdict was read to be on the jury. Most of them seemed to be on your side. You could also try to get a lot of poor, sick people. They'd probably vote for you, especially if you told them you had three children to care for. Especially if they were women. They'd probably understand. They wouldn't send a woman with children back to prison. They would probably try to get her home to her kids as soon as possible. But I guess it's all relative.

What do you mean the divorce is final? I never believed my parents would actually get divorced. Why didn't you just say you're sorry so we wouldn't have to go through all of this? Why didn't someone tell me that you were really, truly divorced? Daddy can't be in Hawaii with anyone else, because he didn't want to divorce you. He said he'd take you back. He just wanted you to realize the consequences of the choices you'd made. He wanted you to apologize and come back home and live the way we were living before, with Daddy as the pastor and you as the wife and us as the kids. You must be wrong. He's probably in Hawaii for church business, not a vacation. If he were going on vacation, he would have brought us kids along. And who is Peggy? I've never even heard of her!

This is too much stress, Mom. First you get charged with a serious crime, then Dad files for divorce, then I have to move to a farm where there is no Internet or phone service, then I have to get used to a new family, then you get sent to prison, then I have to get enrolled in a new regular school in a new town that hardly has any buildings in it. Tomorrow, Sheryl is taking all of us to town for school shopping. Um, I thought we'd be out of here before school. And also, *I hope* she doesn't expect me to dress like her or like June Bug. Their look is just a little too hoochie for me. Don't say I'm being mean, because I'm not. In fact, I've sort of gotten used to having them around. If nothing else, Stretch's mood is a hundred times better when they are here.

Before you go to prison for good, will you send the rest of my Zombie Cowboy series? At the end of book two, Patience Lonelyheart discovers that Handle Boomton is descended from a long line of vampires and that's the reason he's only seen prowling at night. I am embarrassed to admit that I missed so many clues that are now so obvious. He made his money by gambling in the saloons at night. He had pointy teeth. He wore black from head to toe. Anyway, now Patience Lonelyheart and Eamon Cloversniffer have to figure out a way to prevent the marriage, which is taking them a long, long time and many, many pages to figure out. It's a very complicated plot.

Signed,
Penelope

Dear Daddy,

Thank you very much for the postcard from Hawaii. Boy, this is such a surprise! Peggy's swimsuit is very colorful. Yes, I agree that God works in mysterious ways, but I am not sure that Peggy applying for the church accountant position means that God was putting her before your eyes to take as your wife. That's really mysterious, probably a little too mysterious for it to be God's work. But you are the minister and would know more about those signs than me, I guess. Yes, I am taking good care of the boys. Yes, I can see that it will certainly be handy to have a wife who is also in charge of the accounting at the new church. It's hard to believe that Peggy is an accountant, though! Is she a real accountant? Has she gone to college? At first, I thought that was a picture of you with a waitress or something!

Pauly really wants you to call. I checked my phone the last time I was in town, and there weren't any messages from you. Maybe you've called or texted but my phone just isn't receiving the messages? I also checked my email at the library (which is run by a Catholic nun), but I couldn't find any emails from you, either. I checked the junk folder and spam folder, too. But, my email's been acting funny, so maybe I just accidentally deleted your messages. Anyway, Pauly really, really wants you to call, text, email, or come and see us so we can talk about all of this. Especially since Mom can take classes in prison, and I'm sure they offer accounting classes there, too, and she'd probably be more than happy to get an accounting certificate and be your new church's accountant, if that's what you wanted. She's much more agreeable than she used to be. You should call or visit her or send a letter and find out for yourself!

Sincerely,
Penelope

Chapter 9

Percy Versus Penny

IT'S NEARLY IMPOSSIBLE to get some privacy around here. Since I stay in the granary, away from everybody else, I have a little bit—like a tiny, teensy-weensy bit, a bit about as big as one half of one piece of sand—but I still have to use the bathroom in the house just like everybody else, and that bathroom is *not* private. Maybe it used to be, but since the lock on the door's jiggly handle is broken, there's basically no privacy at all. Of course, I found this out the hard way when Penny came barging in as I was drying off after my shower earlier this morning. I was brushing my teeth, and I didn't have my towel around me since I like to let things air out so they don't get too itchy or sweaty before I put on my clothes. Unfortunately, that gave Penny the chance to see pretty much everything, which I swore I wasn't going to show to anyone ever until I got married on my wedding night. To make it worse, Penny started laughing like a jerk before I slammed the door on her stupid face, and then I heard her telling whoever was out in the kitchen about what she just saw.

I've been so ticked off about it that I've been hatching plans of revenge all morning while I paint this little building Uncle Stretch calls the pump house. It's boring work, made even boring-er by the color I have to paint it: white. Come on. If you're going to paint something, at least use some color. The whiteness makes me twitchy, which makes me really want to think of a magnificent revenge for Penny. During a water break, I even ask Elle if she has any ideas, but of course Elle doesn't talk back—she just stands there in her rubber swimsuit, refusing to drop the arm that's covering her breast and chewing her fingernail.

Back at the pump house, I decide I need to set a trap for Penny . . . something that will embarrass and scare her. She really deserves it. As I brush the white paint back and forth, back and forth across the pump house siding, I compose a mental list of things that annoy me about Penny.

1. She has no respect for others' privacy.

2. She wastes all her time trying to decide who to blame for Mom and Dad's problems. First, for a long time, it's all Mom's fault. Then it's Dad's. Then back to Mom. Back to Dad. Mom. Dad. Mom, Dad, Mom, Dad. Momdadmomdad-momdad. Who cares whose fault it is! Move on!

3. She thinks she knows how to interpret the Bible when it's obvious no one really knows how to interpret that book—I mean, it's like two thousand pages long!

4. She thinks she's like Jesus but then is mean to people like Sheryl and June Bug just because she's jealous they look way better than she does. I'm more like Jesus than she is, just based on my humbleness alone. And I don't talk about Jesus stuff all the time like she does. Do you think Jesus went around talking about himself all the time? He would have irritated a lot of people.

5. She is always living in the past. *Percy, do you remember that time in Africa? Percy, do you remember that time in the Philippines?* Hey, Penny, remember that time you were supposed to shut up?

6. She is taller than me.

7. She is a couple of minutes older than me.

8. She is not a boy. At least most twins get a twin who looks and acts like them.

9. She's very uncoordinated and will never be good at sports.

10. The sound of her voice is like one of those swings at a park that squeaks because it's all old and worn-out. *EEK! ERK! EEK! ERK!* Imagine what Penny's voice will sound like when she's old! *EEEEK! ERRRRRK! EEEEK! ERRRRRK!*

All this thinking about Penny's voice actually makes me cover my ears, and when I do that, the paintbrush drips a bunch of white paint onto my cheek. I drop the brush and use my shirtsleeve to wipe the paint off my face. I decide I need to start drawing out these plans instead of thinking. Thinking stresses me out. Drawing relaxes me. I slap some paint on the last side of the pump house, duck my head under a stream of cool water from the nearby pump, and then run to the granary. I grab up my sketchbook and begin to draw out some ideas.

The first plan I draw is for a water balloon launcher that will launch about thirty water balloons at one time from my window in the granary right in through her window in the house. It's about half a football field away, so the balloons would have to go a good fifty yards. They would drench Penny, and if she was wearing her nightshirt, the water would soak her enough that you could see right through the material, and anyone who was watching would pretty much see her naked. But I don't have any wood and a metal spring like I need to build the right kind of launcher. Plus, it would take too long to build. Next, I draw a plan for her to step in a rope and get swooped upside down so she would be hanging from a tree branch. If she was upside down long enough and swinging by her foot from the rope and wearing loose enough clothes, her shirt and shorts might get pulled off by gravity, so that people watching could see her naked, or at least her underwear or stupid bra, which she doesn't even need, by the way, but is always trying to talk about. If she got swooped up when was wearing tight clothes, which she does a lot, it wouldn't work that well. I move on to drawing a blueprint of the bathroom, where I could plant secret cameras in strategic places and then just press record on the cameras and let them run for twenty-four hours. But then I suppose it would record Pauly and Uncle Stretch and Sheryl, too, and I definitely would not want to see any of their bare nakedness. I really don't want to see Penny's at all, either. I just wish she wouldn't have seen mine! I start on a new idea dealing with stealing all her clothes and cutting holes in them, when Pauly walks into my room with a football in his hands.

"How many times have I told you to use the secret knock before entering this room?" I say.

"Hey, P.P.," he says. "I hohd Penny saw you doing a funny naked dance and singing like cwazy into yoh toothbwush like it was a micwophone when you woh in fwont of the mih-woh in the bathwoom."

"What are you talking about?" I say. "That's not true!"

"She told all of us at the bwekfast table she saw yoh ding-a-ling, dude."

"She didn't see a dang thing!" I yell. "Now get out of my room!"

"It's not weally yoh woom, P.P. It's the gwain-o-wee."

"Leave!" I say.

He walks toward the door, then turns around. "You shoh you don't want to play some catch?" he says, tossing the football from hand to hand.

"Where did you even get that football!"

"Stwetch gave it to me. It's one of his old ones."

"Get out!" I scream. I jump off my bed and move toward him like I'm going to cream him, and he runs out of there.

Boy, one thing is for sure. Penny is going down. Forget embarrassing her. I'm going to make her miserable. I'm going to make her wish I was the only one born on our birthday.

I spend nearly all afternoon trying to catch one of the rabbits in this rabbit family I've seen behind the granary the past few weeks. I've got a cardboard box propped up by a stick that has a long piece of string tied to it, which I've been holding, ready and waiting, for when one of the rabbits looks under the box at the stack of carrots I've piled up to lure it. I didn't even go into the house for lunch because I need to get my vengeance as soon as possible.

Catching a rabbit is part two of my plan. There are three parts. Part one was finding just the right Bible verse to use to slam Penny for her sins against me. It didn't even take long since my personal Bible has this appendix in the back that shows you where to find verses based on any word. You can even choose a word like *lamb* or *sexuality* or *homosexuality*, or *murder*, and it will give you the perfect choice of verses. When I chose *vengeance*, I just looked at the first verse they suggested, and bingo, there was a real good one. I have committed it to memory.

Part three involves a big wad of bubble gum.

Out in the yard, one of the rabbits has gotten close to the box a few times, but right before it goes in for the carrots, it looks right at me and—even though I am completely silent and frozen stiff—it's like it can smell me or something because its nose starts twitching. It knows something is up, and it hops away.

After a while, Pauly comes up and asks what I'm doing.

"Quiet, you idiot!" I whisper fiercely. "Obviously, I'm trying to catch a rabbit."

"Sowwy," says Pauly. He hunches down beside me. "Why awe you twying to catch a wabbit?" he whispers, or I should say *sort of* whispers since he's too uncoordinated to really whisper correctly.

"None of your business."

He sits there with me a while, since I decide not to kick him out of there because I'm thinking of using him to trap the rabbit. It takes a little extra thinking, since trying to catch wild animals means you usually have to be smarter than them. I tell this to Pauly and he whispers, "These wabbits awe pwobably smaw-toh than you, P.P."

"Well," I say, "a worm is smarter than you. Even the dumbest worm around."

"That doesn't both-oh me," he says. "I don't weally cay-oh because I like wohms. They'oh pwetty fun to play with, actually."

That gives me an idea. "Okay, here's the plan, Worm Boy," I say. "You need to sneak back to the house and get some of those gross granola bars Uncle Stretch keeps in that one cupboard. You know what I'm talking about?"

Pauly nods his head yes. "I think those gwanola baws are pwetty tasty."

"Whatever," I say. "Just grab a couple and hustle back here. And be quiet! Now go!"

He crawls off on all fours. I don't know why he thinks he has to crawl—what can I say, he's not a smart guy—so it takes him extra long to make it across the yard to the house, but in a few minutes, he's back with the granola bars. I open them and tell him to go sit next to the box and crumble the granola bars into his lap and quietly wait for the rabbits and then try to lure them under the box.

It doesn't take five minutes before three squirrels are creeping up on Pauly. The dummy doesn't even see them at first because he's looking off into the clouds, spacing out about something moronic, I'm sure. Before I know it, all three squirrels are scurrying around Pauly, eating the granola he's spread out. He looks at me and smiles. I give him a thumbs-up and then make a gesture for him to trap one of them under the box, but the confused look on his face shows that he doesn't get what I mean. Two rabbits even pop up out of nowhere and start hopping close to Pauly, but the squirrels see them and one of them starts squeaking a bunch of gibberish. It's pretty funny, because the squirrel's chattering gets louder and louder, and I bet if I could speak squirrel, I would hear some filthy squirrel language with tons of swear words. Whatever the squirrel says makes the rabbits turn right around and hop away. Pauly is chuckling and petting one of the other squirrels as it greedily chomps away at the granola.

I decide that a squirrel will work just as well as a rabbit, and I make my move. With the stealth of a Greek warrior, I sneak up next to Pauly and the squirrels, pick up the cardboard box that's hovering over the pile of carrots, and slam it upside down over one of the squirrels. The other two squirrels jump and scatter, one of them climbing right up Pauly's shirt and then jumping like a madman off Pauly's big, old, stupid head. But the one under the box is trapped. I've got my wild animal!

"Hey!" yells Pauly. "What awe you doing? I was going to twain them to be my pets!"

"Pauly," I say, "you fulfilled your duty, and for that I thank you."

"But that one in the box is pwobably weally scay-ohd."

Pauly is probably right, since the box I'm holding over the trapped squirrel is being thumped and scratched against. I have to make Pauly help me transfer the squirrel into a more secure cage without letting it get away.

"Pauly," I say, "I'll let you keep Nutty to train as a pet if you help me do one little thing first."

I don't even have to explain what the thing is before Pauly says, "Okay."

* * *

Penny's life is pretty dull. I should know, because after I put the squirrel in the cage, I started spying on her. All she's done is read a book outside, by a tree for about an hour, go into the house to get an apple, go back outside to the same tree she was sitting by before, read the same book some more, eat the apple, stare up into the clouds for a while, and then go into her room to write in her notebook. Lucky for me she also has the radio on because Nutty the squirrel, who I now have trapped in a smaller shoe box—an operation that took Pauly and me quite a while to pull off after I was done spying—is clawing at the cardboard, making a tiny racket. I wait a couple of more minutes before I decide that now is the time for action. I push the door open, hiding the shoe box behind my back.

When she sees me, she gets a big smile on her face. "Hey," she says. She covers her mouth to stop a chuckle. "Make up any new dance moves since this morning?"

"Have you ever read Isaiah 34:8?" I bellow.

"What?"

"Isaiah chapter thirty-four, verse eight. 'For the Lord has a day of vengeance, and a year of retribution, to uphold Zion's cause!'"

"What are you talking about?" she says. "And what's in your mouth and what're you hiding behind your back?"

"I'm talking about vengeance," I say.

"If this is about me accidentally seeing you naked this morning, you should just get over it, Percy. We were naked together in the womb for nine months."

"I don't remember that, and neither do you!" I say.

"Actually, I think I do remember some of that time."

"That's a bunch of Horse Camp, Penny!"

"No, it's not. What's Horse Camp is you denying our bond and acting like we're strangers half the time."

"What are you talking about?"

"I think you might have some prepubescent issues you need to deal with about the advent of body changes," says Penny. "It would probably be healthiest for you to take a proactive approach to reconciling the coming changes, both mentally and physically, otherwise you could find yourself acting out without even really understanding why you're doing it."

I don't know what to say, so I just repeat my verse more loudly this time: "*For the Lord has a day of vengeance, a year of retribution, to uphold Zion's cause!*" I then yell a loud *"Ha-ha!"* and release Nutty the squirrel by presenting the shoe box from behind my back and flipping open the top.

It's better than I could've dreamed. Nutty takes a flying jump out of the box and lands on Penny's bed. Penny screeches and the squirrel does, too, as he scrambles across her lap and—I swear—runs right up her wall. He flips upside down in the air and lands on her dresser top, where he knocks over a bunch of perfume and junk. Penny screams again, and it's at this point that I take the big wad of bubble gum I'd been chewing—all five pieces from a pack of watermelon Hubba Bubba—out of my mouth and mush it deep into her hair before repeating my verse one last time at the top of my lungs, slipping out of the room, and blockading the door with a chair before running down the stairs and out of there.

I do a victory leap. I have tamed a wild beast and executed my mission of revenge. I have upheld the cause of Zion and defended the rights of my personal privacy. Now I just hope the squirrel is so scared he poops under her bed and that then it takes her, like, another two weeks to figure out where that bad little smell is coming from. Vengeance is truly mine. *Ha-ha!*

Chapter 10
PENNY VERSUS PERCY

DEAR OKONKWO,

I'M ENCLOSING A PICTURE OF ME WITH MY
NEW HAIRCUT. DO YOU LIKE IT? I MEAN, IF I
WERE A GIRL IN YOUR VILLAGE, WOULD YOU
STILL THINK I AM PRETTY OR ATTRACTIVE? DO
BOYS IN YOUR VILLAGE CARE ABOUT LOOKS THAT
WAY OR DO YOU JUST MARRY THE GIRL WHO
CAN MAKE THE BEST YAM PASTE OR PEANUT
SOUP? IN THE VILLAGE I LIVED IN, THE MOST
MARRIAGEABLE GIRLS WERE THE ONES WHOSE
FATHERS OWNED LOTS AND LOTS OF GOATS. NOW
THAT YOU HAVE YOUR OWN GOAT, YOU PROBABLY
DON'T WORRY ABOUT THAT TOO MUCH AND ARE
MORE INTERESTED IN THE PRETTY GIRLS.

DID YOU KNOW THAT IN THE UNITED STATES, MOST BOYS PREFER GIRLS WITH REALLY LONG HAIR? I IMAGINE THAT SINCE YOU'RE SO POOR YOU CAN'T AFFORD A TV OR INTERNET TO DISCOVER THINGS LIKE THAT. IF YOU CAN'T, DON'T FEEL BAD. I DON'T REALLY HAVE A TV RIGHT NOW, EITHER. NOT ONE THAT I CAN WATCH, ANYWAY, SINCE IT ONLY GETS TEN CHANNELS THAT ARE ALL LOCAL AND SHERYL BASICALLY HOGS IT THE WHOLE DAY.

SHERYL IS MY UNCLE'S GIRLFRIND, WHO BASICALLY LIVES HERE AND TRIES TO BE MY MOTHER. I SUPPOSE IT'S KIND OF LIKE IN YOUR COUNTRY WHERE THE MEN HAVE SIX OR SEVEN WIVES AND THE KIDS HAVE TO LISTEN TO ALL OF THEM, NOT JUST THEIR REAL MOTHER. WE HAVE SOME STATES HERE WHERE A MAN CAN MARRY A MAN, TOO. DO YOU HAVE THAT IN AFRICA? I USED TO THINK THAT KIND OF MARRIAGE WAS A BIG SIN, BUT I'M NOT SO SURE ANYMORE.

HOW'S YOUR GOAT?

PENELOPE PRIBYL

Dear Diary,

Sheryl gave me a haircut, which actually turned out pretty nice, even though I miss my long, long, nice hair that everyone used to compliment and want. Everyone always told me how pretty it was, and now I'll probably only get compliments about my eyes or something like that.

You're probably wondering why I cut my hair if it was so nice in the first place. Well, I did it because Percy's turning into a complete psycho, all because I accidentally saw him dancing and singing naked in the bathroom. If Percy doesn't want people seeing him naked, he should do what I do, which is to undress and dress as quickly as possible and always have your next outfit or towel ready before you strip naked. Also, when I'm in the bathroom, I put the heavy footstool against the door, which Percy definitely did not do.

I hardly even saw any part of him at all, but I told the rest of the family that he was standing there buck naked in front of the mirror, holding a toothbrush like a microphone, and singing into it. He can't even take a little joke and took it way too personally and got me back *twice,* which is not fair. First, he told everyone that I don't even need a bra, which is definitely a lie because I do, and he told everyone that I put cotton balls in my bra to make my chest look bigger, which I did only once, just to see what it looked like. I don't know how Percy could even know that unless he was being a creepy spy, which wouldn't surprise me at all. So that was the first way he got me back.

The second way he got me back was worse. He trapped this squirrel and released it in my room. It could easily have had rabies and bitten me and then he'd be guilty of killing, too. He's totally lucky that I don't turn him in to the authorities for attempted murder. If I had, he'd be in juvie hall sharing a shower with like a hundred other people, all staring at each other's privates. And then what would he do? Come up with crazy plans with squirrels for everyone who saw his privates? Every day? There aren't enough squirrels in the entire state of Minnesota for that.

One time when Mom got mad at Daddy and yelled at him and called him all kinds of foul insults like liar and manipulator and thief and wolf in sheep's clothing, he smiled at her real nicely and said, *Rage is a sin, but I forgive you*. I wish I had remembered to say that when Percy smashed that gum in my hair. Instead, I screamed, and who can blame me? I couldn't stop screaming. I'm embarrassed about all that screaming, but I couldn't help it at all. When I went to Stretch and Sheryl, it was like they didn't know what to do about it. Sheryl covered her mouth and said, "Oh, honey," and Stretch just rubbed his chin. If I get the opportunity, I am going to tell Percy that rage is a sin but I forgive him just like Dad told it to Mom. I think Percy definitely inherited Mom's rage, but I'm not holding a grudge. One nice thing about forgiving someone is that it gives you the upper hand and makes you the better person.

Sheryl works at the hair salon in town, and when I couldn't get the gum out, she told me I'd best get it cut. I didn't want to give Percy the satisfaction of seeing me upset, so I just acted like I've been planning to get my hair cut the whole time. Sheryl brought home a book with lots of pictures of different hairstyles, and I chose one that looks kind of spunky yet classy. I resisted her pleadings that I color it lighter, because my hair is the perfect color already, and I'm never going to change it. In the sunlight, it looks just like a really pretty dark brown color that's hard to describe but is really pretty. Even June Bug said the haircut flattered my face, which is heart shaped and looks good with just about any hairstyle, anyway. She came into my room when we got home from town.

June Bug: (Opening my door.) Knock, knock! Are you okay, Penny?

Me: Yes. I'm fine. I'm better than fine. I'm great.

June Bug: What Percy did was really mean and immature. But it turned out okay because I think you look so mature with your new hair!

Me: Really?

June Bug: Yes, definitely. You look so much older

now. I think you could pass for sixteen or seventeen, at least.

Me: Do you think so? For real?

June Bug: Yes, I just love it. You're so lucky. You have a face shape that suits any haircut.

I have to admit that June Bug can be quite nice and that I like having her around sometimes. I find myself changing my mind about some things lately, which is weird because I try so hard to be right in the first place. It's hard to admit to yourself that you might not always be 100 percent right.

Dear Mom,

Percy stuck gum in my hair on purpose, and I had to have it cut out, so now I have short hair like yours. I'm so depressed! You know how nice my long hair was! I can't stand it here, and I'm really mad that you disintegrated our nuclear family and that you're probably going to spend the rest of your life in jail and that Daddy had to go and find a new wife to replace you. How could you do that to me?

Other than that, I've just been busy cleaning up around here. Pauly had a little cold last week, which may or may not have been a reaction to all the allergens on this farm, and believe me, there are lots! There's horsehair and pollen and hay dust and dust mites and feathers and lots of other things that people are allergic to. I suggested we take him to the doctor in town, but Stretch just said it was a little summer cold and that he'd get over it, like he knows everything there is to know about health. Anyway, I've been trying to keep things extra-clean just in case it is allergies.

Sheryl said that I was nice to have around in the house because I'm so helpful, which was a nice compliment, I thought. Especially since I can see that she's not what I would call the world's greatest housekeeper. Like she doesn't mind if people wear their shoes in the house and only dusts the tops of things once in a great, great while. But I'm going to try to keep helping her because I can see that she gets almost no help from June Bug, who hates to be in the house at all and doesn't think a thing of hanging out in the smelly horse barn for hours and then coming in the house and sitting on the couch or covering up with a clean blanket. It's like she doesn't even consider that she smells and that she's spreading that smell to everything! She can be really dense sometimes. So I try to help Sheryl, who's been extra-tired lately, too. She probably is anemic since she doesn't eat much meat these days and acts like she's going to gag if she sees a chicken cutlet or ground beef. Everyone around here is so dramatic.

Anyway, instead of spreading my hair around the vegetable plants, Sheryl said it was too nice and took it to her church, St. Anthony's Catholic church, in town because they partner up with the beauty salon to donate to Locks of Love. Isn't it strange that Sheryl's a religious person? I didn't even know that because it's not like she goes to church or anything. When I asked her about it, Sheryl said she's a Christmas and Easter kind of Catholic, that she only goes along with the parts of the religion she likes, such as sharing with the poor.

Sheryl: Catholics don't advertise their religion too much. (She says it in a way that makes me think that she thinks that I might advertise my religion a little too much, which I definitely do not!)

Me: (I get a little defensive.) Don't Catholics think that fornication is a sin?

Sheryl: (Her cheeks turn red, probably from anger, which is one of the seven deadly sins, or maybe from embarrassment.) Why, yes, Penny. They do. But I personally believe that some of the rules don't reflect modern culture. What if we all had to live by the cultural practices of biblical times. Would you want that?

Me: How do you know that's not just an excuse to sin? (I stay quiet after that to let the power of my words sink in with her.)

Sheryl: One good thing about Catholics is that they

are generally harder on themselves than they are on other people.

Me: What's that supposed to mean?

Sheryl: They judge themselves before they judge others. They turn their abhorrence for sin inward instead of outward. In my opinion, having personal guilt is way better than being righteously indignant toward everyone else's sins.

Sometimes I'm amazed at the words Sheryl knows. Like, if you look at her, you would never guess that she was smart enough to know the word *righteously* or *indignant*, much less use them together! Anyway, I plan to dictionary.com that phrase the next time I'm at the library.

Love,
Penny

Chapter 11

Percy and Violence

AFTER MY morning chicken-training session, I'm on the riding lawn mower when I drive over some walnuts and one shoots out the grass-blower part and almost hits Pauly, who's trying to capture caterpillars or something over by this big tree. He doesn't even notice.

"Look out, you crazy idiot!" I yell at him.

He doesn't even turn around—just keeps scraping at tree bark with a big glass jar I saw him stealing out of the cupboards earlier this morning. He probably can't hear me over the mower, which sounds like an entire football stadium, if all the fans in it were big fat men with beards who were grumbling because they just got up in the morning. The mower's probably broke, but that's the way a lot of stuff seems here on Uncle Stretch's farm. Either broke or too old-fashioned to work right.

Uncle Stretch made me mow the lawn, something he usually does, to give me an extra chore as punishment for my revenge thing against Penny yesterday. Funny she didn't get punished for walking in on me in the bathroom. Funny Pauly doesn't get punished for being so annoying. Whatever. I keep riding and try to stay away from the walnuts, which isn't easy. It's almost like this car video game I used to have in which you've got to avoid bombs and other cars on the road but you still have to try to speed in order to win. I veer off into a big overgrown patch of grass and weeds in a part of the yard nobody ever uses. I start writing my name in cursive with the mower. I do the *P* and the *E* but the *R* gets kind of messed up because the mower doesn't turn very sharp. I make the *C* and the *Y*, anyway and start thinking it looks pretty cool when Uncle Stretch comes out the front door, sees me and my work, and shakes his head at me.

I get back to work mowing straight lines over my name. I don't mind riding that mower. A four-wheel ATV would be more fun, but of course Uncle Stretch doesn't have one. I asked him why once, and he said, "That's what my horses are for."

Whatever.

Eventually, June Bug runs out to me and points to the house and yells at me though I can't hear. I can tell by the way her lips move that one of the words she's yelling is *lunch*. I shut down the lawn mower and tell her I don't feel like eating with everyone else. She says I should at least take a break, so I say all right and tell her I'm going to be in the granary, relaxing with my thoughts.

"Maybe I could bring you some lunch out there," she says.

"Whatever," I say.

When I get up to my room in the granary, I start feeling bad all over again about Mom and Dad. I try not to think about them much, but the whole situation bugs me. I don't really even believe Dad got remarried—wasn't he still married to Mom? I thought divorces took longer to finalize, but it's hard to know what's actually happening a world away. And Mom's jail thing bugs me the most. I think about how I feel like I'm in jail here on Uncle Stretch's farm, and then I think of Mom being somewhere that's probably five times worse than this farm, a place where she doesn't even get to wear her own clothes or eat food that tastes decent. She probably gets lonely and wishes she had a friend or someone to talk to. I wonder if people are mean to her or if she cries, and that gets me crying.

I go over to the picture of Elle. "My mom's in jail,"

I tell Elle. "That's why I'm sad. I'm not a wimp or anything."

Elle doesn't say anything, of course, but she looks like she understands. I wish we could hug, maybe even kiss. So I kiss the picture. I wonder what Elle's mom is like. "She's probably beautiful like you," I say. "My mom is beautiful, too."

It makes me upset to think of my beautiful mother in a dirty, scary jail where there are people who murdered other people living right next to her. I go over and grab a few extra horse blankets and pile them on top of myself and just sit there and bawl for a while. I imagine Elle crying along with me, but because there's a big ocean in the picture behind her and since she's wearing a swimsuit, people just assume she's been swimming and has ocean water on her face, not tears. I wish I could jump in an ocean.

When June Bug shows up with a sack of food, I stop crying pretty quick and stand up. She smiles at me and takes out a sandwich. The good thing about my mom going to jail is that everybody's been nicer to me after I started crying when we all watched that news show. They think I'm all fragile or something, which is what I heard Sheryl whispering.

"Feeling bad?" asks June Bug. Her skin is so brown now from the summer sun, she looks like Pauly. A cute version of Pauly, that is, since Pauly's weird looking. Not that I think June Bug's cute or anything. I'm just saying that even though she's got a short, boy-like haircut and lots of freckles and looks kind of tough, she looks like a decent girl. She has girl eyes and long eyelashes. She has a soft smile. Not that I'm really looking at her.

I wipe my eyes. I don't say anything back. She'll probably be even nicer to me if I act more hurt than I really am. I take a couple of deep breaths in the shaky way people who've been crying a long time do.

She throws the sandwich at me and says, "Bologna."

"Thanks," I say, not even mentioning I hate bologna.

June Bug takes out a sandwich for herself and starts eating it. "Gimme one of them blankets you've got over there," she says.

"They've probably got horse crap on them," I say.

"Or cat pee," she says. "Just give one, anyway."

I throw her one and she props it against a wall and leans back against it. "Or dog drool," I say.

"Or mad cow disease," she says.

"Or avian bird flu," I say.

She pretends to lick the blanket. "Mmm," she says, "tastes like rabies."

I snort at that one. "You sure it doesn't taste like goat hair?" I say, which turns out not to be that funny.

June Bug examines the blanket up close. "I think I see some bull boogers," she says.

I laugh good at that one, but I can't think of anything more. I blurt out, "It's probably got some of Roland's butt germs on it," but then I wish I hadn't.

June Bug doesn't laugh. "That's sorta mean," she says.

She's right, but I don't like her telling me that. It's quiet for a minute, and then June Bug starts talking chicken. She can talk about them all day, and sometimes does. While some of the stuff is interesting, my mind wanders off, and I just nibble at my dumb sandwich and say nothing for a while.

Somebody comes clomping up the stairs. It's Pauly, and he's got that stupid red Kool-Aid ring on his upper lip again. I think it's always there because even when he's not drinking Kool-Aid, he's licking his lips. He's wearing the new cowboy boots that Uncle Stretch bought for him.

"Hey, guys," he says. "Can I play with you?"

"God, Pauly!" I say. "We're not playing!"

"Easy, Percy," says June Bug.

Pauly walks across the room to the exercise bike I fixed up enough so you can actually pedal it. I've been working out on it every other day. He looks at it, and then hops on. "Can I twy it?" he asks and starts pedaling.

"If you break that, I swear I'm going to kill you!" I say to him.

"Percy!" says June Bug.

Pauly can't really reach the pedals right, so he nudges forward off the seat and stands on the pedals. He starts cycling them with his boots, but he looks like Carl the chicken trying to run fast but not doing it. Some metal starts scraping and just like that, one of the pedals falls off and so does Pauly. The bike crashes over on its side.

"You idiot!" I say and spring over to where Pauly's lying. I punch him in the head, and when he covers it, I punch him in the guts and when he covers those, I go for the head again. "Idiot!" I yell. "I told you not to break it!" I rear back for another punch but before I can swing, I get bowled over by a big horse blanket swung by June Bug. I go rolling but get up fast and come at her. I take a swing at her, but she ducks and the next thing I know, her fist is blasting me in the stomach and taking all my air away. I fall to my knees. I can't take a breath, and it feels like I'm dying. June Bug pushes me all the way down and sits on my chest, pinning my arms with her knees. I don't even try to fight back because I can barely breathe!

"C'mere, Pauly," she says.

Pauly gets up and runs over. He's not crying or anything, just rubbing his head where I punched him.

"Go ahead, Pauly," says June Bug. "Punch your brother in the face."

"Weally?" says Pauly.

I scream, "He's not even my brother!" Then Pauly's little fist thumps me in the eye.

"Oww!" I say. "Let me up, June Bug!"

"Punch him harder," says June Bug.

"I weally don't want to," says Pauly.

"Fine," says June Bug. I think she's going to let me up, but then I see her hand moving quickly, and then I feel it stinging my face. "That's for trying to hit a girl," she says. She slaps me in the face again, harder. "That's for treating everyone around here like crap," she says.

It hurts, and I feel like crying, but I also feel embarrassed, so I don't. I'm probably in shock.

"Let me up!" I say.

She slaps me again.

"Let me up!" I scream. "Let me up!"

She sits there, looking at me. "Stop taking out your problems on everyone else. You don't have a mom and a dad here? So what? I don't have a dad around, either. Pauly's parents abandoned him when he was a baby. Stretch lost his son. You're not the only one with problems."

"I hate you!" I say. "I hate being here! I hate this place!"

Above me, June Bug pulls her hand back again. Then she drops it. "This place isn't so bad, Percy. Your life isn't so bad."

"Get off me!"

Out of nowhere, a cowboy boot kicks me in the mouth. It feels like my lips and teeth have exploded.

"Pauly!" yells June Bug.

She finally gets off me. I roll over, and blood is gushing out of my mouth. I can taste the blood, and my tongue feels something else in my mouth. I spit on the floor and out comes something white—a tooth!

"Oh, no!" says June Bug.

I look at Pauly. He covers his mouth with his hand. "Sowy, Pohcy," he says.

I pick up the tooth and run my tongue around my mouth. There's a hole where one of the top two teeth should be.

"Lift up your lip," says June Bug. "Smile at me."

I feel like punching rather than smiling, but I do what she says.

"Whoa," she says. "Your front tooth is gone."

I don't know what to do, so I just sit down on the horse blankets. There's blood all over my shirt and hands now, and my whole head feels like a giant heart-beat. It hurts, but I'm not crying.

"You don't look so good," says June Bug. "There's gonna be trouble."

Chapter 12
PENNY'S MANY MOODS

Dear Diary,

Now that Percy's front tooth is out, he looks like a hillbilly and makes a really annoying whistling sound when he laughs. Not only that, but there's something going on behind my back. One minute, Percy hates Pauly and can't wait to insult or hit him. Next, they're in Percy's room in the granary with June Bug, doing God knows what. And then Percy comes out missing his front tooth, and Pauly's staring at his new boots, and when I ask what happened, they all look at each other and start laughing like it's the funniest thing they've ever heard. Then Percy ruffles Pauly's head and says that he tripped over a horse blanket and knocked out his tooth on the floor. *And*, this is the real kicker: Percy gave the tooth to Pauly to put under his pillow so the tooth fairy brings Pauly money! Has everyone lost their minds?

By the way, here is my mood today: *crabby*!

I'm pretty sure there's something seriously wrong with me, like I might have stomach cancer or an ulcer or twisted bowels. This dull, drumming ache started yesterday while we wrangled those dang chickens into their crates for shipping to the fair. I'm sure it has something to do with Sheryl's cooking, which is all potatoes, beets, radishes, tomatoes, peppers, cucumbers, and everything else that's come right out of the garden and has not been washed properly. Since she's practically moved in and is living in sin with Stretch, I've gained ten pounds!

And my hands look like constellation charts with all the scratches and peck marks from those hens and roosters that most certainly did not want to have anything to do with getting into the crates. I can tell these scratches are about five seconds from getting infected with staph bacteria. Soon they'll be pussing, oozing, and spreading, and then I'll be a candidate for amputation, which I'm sure will be just fine with Stretch, who'd probably love hacking off a limb with a rusty saw or an old pocketknife. Just writing in my diary is opening up the wounds and making them bleed. I don't mind working, but I don't think it's fair for me to risk life and limb just so Percy and June Bug can traipse around the county fair like they're some sort of preteen chicken gurus. They're like, *Ooohh. See how my bird has clean plumage and beautifully layered feathers? See how pertly she holds her head? How red her comb and wattle are? How puffy her breast? How she doesn't pick and peck at her skin like she's got droves of mites and ticks? See how straight and sharp her beak is? Why, she could pluck the eyeball right out of your skull!*

That June Bug. She's really getting on my nerves again, probably because she's practically moved in here, too, along with her mother. I thought for a while that she was pretty cool, but, in all truthfulness, she can be totally annoying. She really thinks she's special. Who cares about chickens?! I happen to know that Percy doesn't know squat about these birds. He says things like, *Uh. Duh. This one has three claws on each leg. Oh. Look, this one laid an egg.* As if laying eggs were comparable to juggling or throwing knives at balloons. Show me a chicken that can do that, and I'll be impressed. I also happen to know that the chickens have no interest in parading their feathers just so those two can get big ribbons strapped to their chests and do *more* bragging. When I told June Bug that the chickens did not want to get in the crates and go to the fair, she told me chickens don't have consciousness or understanding.

June Bug: (Acting like a big know-it-all in her plaid shirt and petting a chicken like she actually cares about it.) Penny, chickens don't reason. Everything they do is because of instinct.

Me: How do you know? Did one of them tell you that?

June Bug: (Looking startled with wide eyes.) Well, no, but I've been around farm animals for my whole life.

Me: Well, I've been around the church my whole life, but I wouldn't run around pretending like I have God all figured out. (I, for one, think that is a really good point.)

June Bug: (Pretending as though she really cares about me.) No, I suppose not. But I'm not sure knowing stuff about God is comparable to knowing stuff about chickens. Penny, are you feeling all right? You don't seem to be yourself today.

She said it like a big know-it-all, and right in front of my brothers because there's nothing she likes better than to try to be the smartest, prettiest, and bossiest one, particularly to me because she's probably intimidated by me. I wouldn't doubt it one bit.

Anyway, I'm not sure that chickens don't think. Like, while I was holding this one chicken, I kind of petted its head and stroked its back while June Bug and Percy made a nest for it in the crate. I held it against my stomach and tried to keep its legs still so it wouldn't claw my intestines out. After a while, it stopped flapping like a lunatic and seemed to rest against me, and it had a look in its eye that didn't seem nervous. I mean, it must relax because it realizes that I'm not going to hurt it, right? Don't those reactions indicate some sort of thinking on the chicken's part? June Bug didn't even consider what I had to say. She just said no and then asked me if I was turning into a vegetarian.

Despite my nice, brief chicken moment, I won't be showing chickens like everyone else around here. Instead, I'm going to do something more original and enter the county fair's talent contest. I'm leaning toward doing a PowerPoint presentation on something educational. Because I'll need a few resources for that, I rode into town yesterday with Sheryl to hang out at the library while she worked. When she asked if I minded if she smoked a little tiny cigarette while we drove, I told her yes, I most certainly did. She respected my opinion and did not smoke in the car, which was probably a personal miracle of self-control on Sheryl's part.

Sister Alice was there being her usual crabby self. She asked me about a million times if she could help me find something. After I told her no, no, and no, she said, "Well, quit pushing in the all the books you touch. I don't like when the books are pushed in. I prefer that all the books are a uniform distance from the edge of the shelf." I pushed in three more and told her, "It's a free country, lady."

Then she said to me, "You want a taste of my wooden spoon?"

I decided not to tell her about corporal punishment being illegal and fixed the books the way she liked them. Sometimes, you just have to let old people have their way.

I found a number of satisfactory medical dictionaries and books on diseases that were quite interesting. I also looked up that phrase, *righteously indignant*. Now I wonder if Sheryl was referring to me when she used it, and that just makes me really mad at how judgmental she was being. I'm going to take a hot bath, and no one better bother me while I'm at it, or I swear I'll go ballistic.

Dear Mom,

You know how you and Dad always said that if you can't say something nice, then you shouldn't say anything at all (though now that I think about it, Dad said not-so-nice things about people all the time, didn't he? If you ask me, he was constantly full of righteous indignation.)? Well, I've got to keep this letter short since I'm in some sort of a funk this week, so I don't have much to say.

Hope you're having a jolly time working on your appeal.

Penny

Dear Dad,

Have you given any interesting sermons lately? Like maybe a sermon on hypocrisy? Does your new wife like listening to you preach? Does she sit where Mom and us kids used to?

Lots of love from Horse Camp, from your daughter, the one you sent to Stretch's farm, the one who always listened to you no matter what, the one who always did whatever you said.

Penelope

Chapter 13

Percy and the Chicken

ON THE FIRST DAY of the weeklong Red Rock County Fair, Uncle Stretch and Sheryl drop us off at the fowl show, and we're led into this big barn with our chickens. I must say it's a bit of a disappointment. The show barn is sort of smelly and dusty, and the seats where I had imagined there would be many people cheering sit empty, which is a bummer. When I visualized my chicken-showing performance earlier this morning, I had counted on a crowd clapping and whistling for me. I always do better in front of a crowd. When I mention this to June Bug, she says only entrants, chickens, and judges are allowed in the judging area, because a couple of years ago, parents were trying to whisper answers to their kids when the judges asked them questions.

So, without anybody making a big deal of it, we hold our chickens in their individual cages and stand before our judges, who sit in a long row of chairs and call us over, one by one. June Bug and Pauly get friendly-looking judges, but I get an old guy who's got a grouchy look.

Trying to stay calm in order to not make my fowl nervous, I take Hercules, my chicken, out of his cage and hand him to the judge, who, first thing, looks at my missing tooth and frowns. For a while now, I've been getting weird looks from people when they see the hole in my smile, but I usually take it as a sign of respect. Uncle Stretch tried ordering me to the dentist, but I wouldn't go. I don't appreciate the judge's frown, since it seems like he respects me less instead of more because of my missing tooth. Then he starts firing questions at me like bullets.

You know how when you've studied something really hard, but when it comes time to prove it, your brain forgets everything? Well, here I am, showing Hercules at the Red Rock County Fair, and this old grumpy judge is asking me chicken questions, and all the sudden it's like I don't know a single thing, even though chickens have been like my family over the past month! Closer than Mom, Dad, Penny, and Pauly. Definitely closer than Uncle Stretch, Sheryl, and June Bug. A couple of times, when I fell asleep in the granary at night, I'd even have chicken dreams. In one of them, I was this old, shabby-looking rooster, like Carl. My legs seemed really slow and creaky, and I could barely make any chicken noises, but I must've been tough because when the other chickens started pecking at me, I flapped my wings and flew around, pecking them back, one by one, until everyone was dead. I didn't realize it was so easy to kill other chickens with your beak, but there they were, lying all bloody and still, with feathers all scattered around. It was a weird dream—but just a dream.

The old judge surveys Hercules and grabs a part of Hercules's neck like his fingers are a tweezers. "Identify," he says.

My brain is so blank, I can't think of anything to say at all! I try to imagine Elle telling me things to say, but even that doesn't work. It's like Elle is just worried about her arm falling down and her breast being out there for everyone to see. Then I start thinking about that, too, and it's like chickens are the furthest thing from my mind. I look down the line at June Bug. Her judge, a smiling older lady, is petting her chicken. I look farther down the line at Pauly's situation, and something has happened there that is so funny that his judge, a white-bearded guy who looks like a Santa Claus, is laughing and slapping his knee!

Hercules is looking nervous, jutting his head around like he is listening to crazy music. I don't think he likes being touched—well, not by the judge, anyway. I chose him because he was the biggest, even though he wasn't the tamest.

"Son," says the judge, waggling Hercules' neck part between his fingers. "That's the wattle." He stares at me like he's superdisappointed and adds, "One of the most *identifiable* parts of *Gallus domesticus*."

"Of what?"

"That's Latin for chicken," he says.

Latin? I think. *I barely know English right now.* "Uh, okay," I say. "Do I lose points for not knowing?"

"Son," says the judge, "you don't have any points to lose yet." He takes up one of my bird's legs with his fingers, but Hercules pulls it away and starts clucking like he's real sick of this junk. The judge grabs again but can't get hold of the leg. "Have you been working with your fowl?" says the judge.

"What do you mean?" I say.

The judge stops trying to grab the leg and instead just makes his hands into a big bowl for Hercules to rest in. Hercules calms down after about thirty seconds, and the judge gives me a look like *See? I know how to treat your bird better than you!* He starts stroking Hercules's head, smoothing his hand all the way down the back feathers. Hercules gets real still. The judge turns Hercules around so his butt is pointing at me.

"Identify the anus," says the judge.

"You mean the butt hole?" I say.

"The *anus*," says the judge sternly.

"With . . . my finger?"

"What else would you use?"

"Uh, I doubt I could find it," I say. "Hercules has got a lot of feathers in that area."

"Identify the anus," says the judge.

"I don't think this chicken has one," I say.

"It's right here," says the judge, his fingers disappearing under Hercules's feathers. He gets a look on his face like you would if you're digging into your pants pocket, searching for change.

Well, you can tell when the judge finds the spot because Hercules lets out a screech and shoots into the air. The judge jumps up, too, to try and grab Hercules, but Hercules beats his wings and hovers there, *Ba-Gock! Ba-Gock!*-ing. I just step back because I've seen chickens get like this before, and it isn't pretty. But the judge won't give up. He keeps lunging for Hercules but missing. Finally, Hercules dives right for the judge's face, clawing and pecking. All the other kids and judges look at us.

The judge's head looks like a snowman's—but with feathers—until finally he grabs Hercules by the neck and slams him down on the ground. Hercules makes a real bad croaking sound, and then lies there, not moving. It's real quiet in the barn. One of the judge's eyeglass lenses has popped out, and his forehead has some bloody scratches on it, and his hair is all messed up with some white-yellow stuff that came from Hercules' anus! Nobody says anything, but you can hear the judge breathing hard. Wheezing.

"What!" he yells, finally. "That fowl tried to blind my eyes!" Then he steps over the body of Hercules and stomps on out of the barn.

Some old guy with a big belly hanging over a shiny belt buckle the size of my hand rushes over to Hercules and sweeps him into a five-gallon pail with a hand broom. "Sorry, kid," he says to me. He tells me to just sit in the bleachers and watch for a while, then he walks off. I don't know where he takes my poor dead chicken, but I'd sure bet it's not to some beautiful chicken cemetery.

When Uncle Stretch asks Pauly, June Bug, and me how the chicken judging went, Pauly and June Bug look right at me. I say that it went just fine. Pauly starts to say something, but then June Bug butts in and says, "Oh, it was fine for us, too. Just fine."

Uncle Stretch tells us to meet them at 5 p.m. at the 4-H food stand, then buys us a bunch of tickets so we can go on rides all afternoon. He and Sheryl are going to watch Loose Change, this local country-western band that has this glass-eyed singer, over in the grandstand. Penny is off wandering by herself.

Though I'm supposed to stick with Pauly and June Bug, I get sick of hearing how great their chickens did at the judging. When we're supposed to be getting on the Ferris wheel together, I act like I gotta go to the bathroom. I tell them I'll meet them when they get off, but instead I just avoid them and ride on the Scrambler twice, the Tilt-a-Whirl four times, and the Bullet nine times. Then I play some games and buy a corn dog and some minidonuts with the five bucks Uncle Stretch gave me. As much as I could go for a big snow cone or a milk shake, my broke-out tooth won't let me eat really cold stuff. It makes me look tougher, though, so I don't mind much.

I ask some old lady what time it is, and she says 5:15, so I hustle over to the 4-H food stand.

When I find everybody, they're all sitting there, eating pie and ice cream. Uncle Stretch gives me a bad look, and I can tell June Bug and Pauly told him about how I ditched them. Uncle Stretch starts in by saying, "So where were you all afternoon?" but Sheryl says, "Oh, Stretch, the boy's here now—let this one go."

Uncle Stretch doesn't want to let it go, I can tell, but he whips out his wallet, fishes out a couple of bucks, and shoves them under my nose. "You go get some pie and ice cream," he says roughly.

I point to my missing tooth. "No ice cream," I say. "Too sensitive."

"Well, pie, then," says Uncle Stretch, slapping the money into my hand.

When I get back, Penny talks and talks about some horse she made a connection with over in one of the barns. June Bug talks about her own chicken so much I don't have to say anything about Hercules. We finish up at the food stand and head over to the grandstand for the results of the chicken judging. It's not a big crowd, but in addition to the kids who showed birds, about twenty of us, some parents, brothers and sisters are there, too. Maybe close to a hundred people in all, including the judges, though my judge is nowhere to be seen.

A man in a cowboy hat and old-fashioned mustache steps up to a podium and says, "I am pleased to announce our five purple ribbon winners and our grand champion in the annual Red Rock County Fair Fowl Show. All participants not awarded purple ribbons or grand champion will be awarded green ribbons for participation. Everyone," he adds with a smile, "is, in some fashion, a champion."

June Bug looks at her mom and rolls her eyes.

"If your name is called, please come up to the podium to receive your ribbon and gather for a photo shoot." He unfolds a paper. "Purple ribbons go to . . . Danny Blanchette, Riley Minion, Sherylynn Johnson, Jeff Juvie, and Buddy Herding."

People applaud, and June Bug gets a big smile.

"Come on up, kids!" the man in the cowboy hat says, and the kids make their way to the stage. Pauly claps hard for June Bug.

"And our grand champion and entrant into the Red Rock County Fair . . . is . . . Perseus Pribyl."

Grand champion? Me? Whoa! I'm running down to the platform before I know what's happening. People are slapping me on the back and shaking my hand and taking my picture and pinning an oversized blue ribbon onto my shirt. Camera flashes make me see stars.

Uncle Stretch and Sheryl and June Bug and Pauly and Penny eventually make their way up to me. Penny gives me a big hug. Uncle Stretch shakes my hand and laughs.

"Wow!" says Sheryl. "Grand champion."

June Bug smirks and shakes her head. "Congratulations," she says.

Pauly says, "What's so gweat about a dead bohd?"

"What dead bird?" asks Uncle Stretch.

I smile my toothless smile, much too caught up in admiring my big blue ribbon to answer such a question.

Chapter 14

PENNY AND THE TALENT SHOW

Dear Diary,

It's a few days before the fair.

Even though the costume component is only worth ten points in the Red Rock County Fair Talent Show, Sheryl and June Bug have been staying up late night after night. They've been running the sewing machine so loud and long that none of the rest of us could get a wink of sleep, in order to put together the tackiest, trashiest country-western outfit ever! June Bug is going to wear a red satin shirt tied up in a knot to bare her midriff (of course!) and a pair of cutoff jean shorts with little balls stitched all around them that look like they were ripped right off some old grandma's lamp shade. When June Bug dances, Sheryl says, the little balls will add extra interest.

Apparently, June Bug's talent is singing. Who told her it was a talent of hers, I have *no* idea. She sounds like a braying calf with a bad case of smoker's cough. Secondhand smoke, now that I think of it, probably *is* the reason June Bug already sounds like she's been hanging out in truck stops for forty years. Anyway, she's been using anything handy as a practice microphone, singing and dancing her Shania Twain routine (welcome back to the 1990s, everyone!) until even Pauly has all the words and the steps memorized. While he was sitting on the toilet this morning, I heard him singing, *I'm gonna gitchoo while I gotchoo in sight. I'm gonna gitchoo if it takes all nigh-yight.* Not a very appropriate song for a kid to be singing, in my opinion.

Sheryl didn't even ask me if I wanted to be in the talent show. She just entered me and left the type-of-performance category blank, so now it's up to me to choose from: vocal solo, vocal duet, vocal group, instrument solo, instrument duet, instrument group, cheer routine, tap, contemporary dance, ballet, interpretive dance (what the heck's that mean?), and other.

I have many talents. I just don't think I need to go around flaunting them in front of a big crowd. But when I protested, Sheryl said sometimes it's good to try things outside our comfort zones. Stretch told me I was going to do it and to stop with the nonsense. I've been here long enough to know that if Stretch says something's going to happen, it's going to happen. In a way, his absolute inability to change his mind about any issue is sort of comforting. It's almost like he's the most reliable adult we've ever had in our lives, but I would never tell him that.

Anyway, I've pretty much resigned myself to the fact that I'm going to be in this talent show and so I'd better make the best of it. I've never danced, really, except for a few times during some of Dad's more lively sermons when the Holy Spirit came down and touched us (or at least that's what *he* said was happening). I can sing. Mostly I just like to sing hymns from church, but I don't feel too good about church or Dad lately, so hymns naturally fall into the not-an-option category. And I'm not about to prostitute myself like June Bug by singing foolish country or pop songs. No, my talents are more intellectual. I'm going to do a PowerPoint presentation on diagnosing a strange or horrible disease. Something practical. So I choose "other" from the type-of-performance list of categories and write in the blank: PowerPoint Presentation on African sleeping sickness.

Red Rock County Fair Talent Show PowerPoint Presentation

African Sleeping Sickness
by Penelope Pribyl

African sleeping sickness is just one disease people should know about before traveling to Africa. A lot of people don't know anything about it until it's *too late*!

1. What is African sleeping sickness?

This deadly disease is caused by a parasite carried by the tsetse fly. Around twenty-five thousand new cases are reported to the World Health Organization each year. Since 1967, thirty-six cases of sleeping sickness have been reported within the United States, all among individuals who had traveled to Africa. They were mainly missionaries who didn't take proper precautions or who thought they are immune against diseases because God would protect them.

2. How is African sleeping sickness spread?

The tsetse fly, although small, sometimes carries around the sleeping sickness parasite, and when the fly bites you, the parasite enters your body and starts killing you.

3. **What are the symptoms of African sleeping sickness?**

A bite by the tsetse fly is often painful and can develop into a red sore, also called a chancre. Fever, severe headaches, irritability, extreme fatigue, swollen lymph nodes, and aching muscles and joints are common symptoms of sleeping sickness. Some people develop a skin rash. Some people start to go crazy, and sometimes villagers mistake sleeping sickness for devil possession or madness and try to chase the poor, infected soul from the village or try to drag the infected person to church so that the preacher can perform an exorcism. If the person is not treated by a real doctor, infection becomes worse and death will occur within several weeks or months.

4. **What should I do if I think I may have African sleeping sickness symptoms?**

First of all, if you live anywhere in the United States, you probably don't have African sleeping sickness and probably shouldn't get too excited if you have some of the symptoms I've listed above. You could possibly have Lyme disease, which has some of the same symptoms and is carried and spread by the bite of a tick. You can die from that, too, so you should go to the doctor. Not many people know this, but President George Bush was treated for Lyme disease. But if you've been to Africa lately and think you may have sleeping sickness, go to the doctor ASAP. You may have to give a blood sample, a spinal tap, and skin biopsies.

5. How can you prevent African sleeping sickness?

A. Wear protective clothing, including long-sleeved shirts and pants. The tsetse fly can bite through thin fabrics, so clothing should be made of thick material. Nobody really does this, though, because it's so hot in Africa.

B. Insect repellent is useless because the tsetse flies don't mind the taste of it.

C. Use bed netting when sleeping, and be sure to nail it down. The little African children love to do nothing better than to steal this netting and take it home to their mothers. The next thing you know is that they've put up the netting over their herds of goats, so the animals don't get sick. Some families value their goats more than their children.

D. Avoid bushes. The tsetse fly is less active during the hottest period of the day. It rests in bushes but will bite if disturbed. Also, a lot of deadly snakes hang out in the bushes.

Red Rock County Fair
Talent Show Judging Form
Judged by Mrs. Alvin Guggisberg, lead judge

Name: Penelope Pribyl

Category: Other—PowerPoint Presentation on African sleeping sickness

Costume: 0/10, candidate appeared to wear her regular clothing and made no attempt to design an attractive or interesting outfit to complement her talent.

Audience Contact: 6/10, candidate did appear genuinely interested in the health of the audience members, but made no attempt to entertain the crowd or otherwise engage the crowd in a pleasing, happy manner. Candidate read directly from her screen, which the audience members were capable of reading for themselves, and made no other additional comments or suggestions or insight into African sleeping sickness.

Stage Presentation: 24/30, candidate did speak and read clearly. She included many flashy tricks in her

PowerPoint presentation, including having the text fade in and out, roll off the screen like in *Star Wars*, and appear magically from either side of the screen. She also varied the font and screen color to add spice to the show! Good job!

Talent Ability: 48/50, candidate knows her stuff! Whoo-wee! I learned a lot, I have to admit. I'm just not sure this type of presentation qualifies as a talent performance (we'll probably have to go over this at the next board meeting). But since this presentation snuck in this year, I have to judge it on its merits, and Ms. Pribyl's ability to diagnose and discuss African sleeping sickness is clear.

Total: 78/100, fourth-place white ribbon and $20 prize

Dear Diary,

Today at the fair, I won fourth place in the talent show! To be honest, I really enjoyed educating all the audience members, even if a lot of them were checking their phones for text messages, and one guy even made a phone call to a woman named Tracy while I was talking. I kept going and didn't let their rude behavior interrupt my train of thought or my mission of ridding the world of this terrible disease. Fourth place is pretty good, but you'll never believe who got first place and one hundred dollars. Yep, June Bug. I think mostly because of the way she kept doing cartwheels and her outfit, which the boys and men in the audience couldn't keep their eyes off of. If she wore that to Africa, the tsetse flies would swarm her like crazy, and she'd be infected with sleeping sickness and be dead before she could even sing one note of Shania Twain. Anyway, Stretch and Sheryl were real proud of June Bug and me and took us all out for hamburgers and shakes. When Percy said that he thought June Bug's act was awesome but mine was kind of boring, Stretch smacked him in the back of the head and told him to shut it. June Bug said that she didn't think my act was boring at all and that she learned a lot. I don't understand that girl very well. She really acts very, very nice, and that confuses me. I'll have to keep my eye on her.

One of the other big events of the fair was the merciless slaying of Percy's fancy chicken by the so-called chicken expert at the Red Rock Fowl Show the day before the talent show. What a total and complete Horse Camp! That first day of the fair after the chicken judging, things were pretty tense when Stretch asked where Percy's chicken was and Percy wouldn't 'fess up. Pauly said it was dead, so that's all we knew, and Sheryl made Stretch calm down until we got home, which she said was the proper place to deal with the situation, not in public. That night before bed, Stretch made Percy spill all the particulars. June Bug and Pauly suddenly remembered vivid details and filled in bits Percy conveniently missed. When Percy told Stretch and Sheryl how the judge manhandled and killed his bird, you could tell Percy didn't even really care. He was just happy to have gotten attention and sympathy for basically bringing a wild chicken to the fair. The fact that the judges most likely made him champion out of the fear of someone suing them went right over Percy's head.

In addition, I was not impressed that Percy included June Bug and Pauly into his little lie of exclusion in not telling what happened until well after the fact. Pauly has surely been traumatized by the whole event. It's not every day that a child is forced to witness the beating to death of a live animal.

As a result of this, I started paying more attention to all the other animals. I have been sitting in the horse barn at the fair, just fellowshipping with all the horses, which are wayyyy better than Bernie and Brenda. There's this one, a black stallion named Mick, who I feel a strong connection to. Just looking at his eyeball, close up, made me wonder at God's creation. Like, how did God (or whoever it was) come up with a horse eye, this thing that's way bigger than a human eye, way smaller than a whale eye, but so beautiful and black that you can see your reflection in it? And to think that

Mick can see with it, can see me, can see the world. It's so complicated, but so marvelous.

Also, I felt a strong connection to Mick's owner, Wesley, who is a year older than me and really handsome, and who called me beautiful. He looks exactly like I have imagined Eamon Cloversniffer looks, except he's not a zombie. Wesley has dark hair, brooding eyes with dark circles under them, and red lips. He tilts his head when he talks like intelligent people do, I have noticed. In chapter four of *Cowboy Zombie, Book Two*, it reads, "Eamon Cloversniffer mounted his mighty steed with grace, tipped the lid of his hat, and tilted his head as if in intelligent thought." That's exactly what Wesley looks like when he's on his horse, Mick.

Chapter 15

Percy Meets Jimmy

IT'S THE LAST full day of the county fair, and I've got pretty much the whole day to kill. Sheryl is taking June Bug and Penny to the adult talent show this afternoon, since they wanted to see it after winning prizes in the kid talent show, which I probably should have entered and won. Uncle Stretch is watching the minirodeo with Pauly. Tonight, there's fireworks and a square dance that Uncle Stretch and Sheryl are all excited about. I suppose I'll see the fireworks, but I don't care about any of that other junk. I'd like to go by myself. Uncle Stretch says, "Here's ten bucks. Don't spend it all on games or rides because you gotta eat on it, too."

"Ten bucks?" I say.

"That's all you get," says Uncle Stretch.

Sheryl reaches into her purse and gives me another five. Uncle Stretch gives her a bad look.

"Thanks," I say.

"Meet us by the John Deere tractors at eight o'clock," says Uncle Stretch.

"Yep," I say and run off.

I play a couple of games of football toss, but I can't win, because either the footballs are too big or they made the holes you were supposed to be able to throw the footballs through too small. Then I play a couple of games of ringtoss and throw-the-dart-at-the-balloon and BB-gun shoot, but I don't do that great at those, either. Maybe I'm just off today.

I'm out of money before I remember to save a little for a corn dog or some minidonuts.

There's nothing to do, so I just walk around and watch people. I walk by all the games I wasted my money on. Then I walk by the food, and the smells make me pretty hungry, so I walk back over by the games. A lot of kids are with their parents. At the knock-over-the-milk-bottles-with-a-baseball, this dad with a curly red Afro is making a fool of himself trying to impress everyone, probably his family. He throws the balls hard but is really wild. He almost hits the guy running the game, who says, "Whoa, whoa, whoa! Do I have to wear a helmet, mister?" Two young boys, who have matching red curly hair, laugh. I'm glad that guy isn't my dad. What a dork.

I briefly wonder what my dad is doing. I remember we once went to a carnival-type thing in the Philippines. It didn't have rides, but there was a fishing contest and my dad won it. It wasn't like he was the best fisherman, though. I think he just got lucky. Or maybe the village elders let him win so he'd think they liked him. My dad's likeable if you go along with him. He's probably got a new group of people liking him already. He moves on quickly. I get that from him, which is why, after Mom got into trouble, I'm handling this whole Horse Camp thing as well as I am.

I walk by the Pop-a-Shot basketball game and see this older kid wearing baggy black jeans with a silver chain dangling from his pocket and a greasy-looking white tank top. He is really awesome at it. He keeps grabbing those minibasketballs and pumping them in the hoop like he is a basketball-shooting machine. It doesn't even matter which hand—left or right—he just flips his wrist into a little gooseneck. *Swish, swish, swish.* He makes about ten in a row before missing one, then he makes about twenty straight after that.

When his game ends, the guy in charge, a short, fat man with his shirt half-unbuttoned, says, "Which one, bud?" and points to the big prizes. "Any one you want with that score."

When the kid turns around, I see he looks about sixteen or seventeen, with bushy black eyebrows and longer black hair and some wispy black hairs on his chin. He sort of has a mustache, too. He looks pretty cool. "Don't want it," he says. He holds out a five-dollar bill. "I want a few more rounds, though."

"Sure, sure," says the guy in charge, and then the kid starts another game, swishing almost every shot. Other people start to watch, too, folding their arms across their chests and smiling. This kid is *amazing* at basketball!

After he plays his last dollar, he pulls a pack of cigarettes out of his pants pocket, pops one out into his hand, and lights it with a black lighter. His hands are superquick. He huffs out a huge gray cloud, and it hangs there a second before he walks away.

I don't know why, but I decide to follow the kid. He walks into a livestock barn, tossing down his cigarette and stomping it out before he goes in. I watch him stop and stare at a cow and its calf. Some young girls act like they're not looking at him, but they are. They all look back at him after they walk by. One of them covers another's mouth with her hand, and they giggle. He just looks at the animals and keeps on walking, lighting up another cigarette as he goes.

I follow him to the edge of the fair where not many people are, and he turns a corner behind a big old barn. I peek around the corner and see him toss away his cigarette and unzip his pants to pee on the side of the barn. I hide my face quick because I don't want him seeing me see that!

After a minute, I hear this thumping sound, and I peek again. The kid is bouncing this old-looking ball against the dirt and dead grass, but the ball is out of air, so it doesn't bounce very well. He shoots it, and I have to lean out farther to see where the ball goes. There's a hoop nailed to the barn wall. The ball goes straight through it—or at least it looks like it does—there's no net. The ball hits the barn wall and thuds to the ground.

"Hey," yells the kid. "Why you been following me?"

I think of running, but I don't. "I don't know," I say. "I was watching you play that basketball game back there. You're really good."

The kid walks over to his flat ball and picks it up. "What do *you* know? What are you, a kindygardner?"

"I'm twelve," I say. "Seventh grade going into eighth."

"So frickin' what?" says the kid. He pounds his ball into the ground, snatches it up when it doesn't bounce back, and shoots again. The ball flies at the hoop, hits the barn wall, and thuds to the ground. Probably a swish. He walks over to it, his pants chain jangling a little, picks the ball up, walks farther away from the hoop than he was before, and shoots again. *Smack, thud.* Walk, walk. *Smack, thud.* Walk, walk. *Smack, thud.* Walk, walk. *Smack, thud.*

I try to think of something cool to say, but I can't, so I just watch for a long time. Finally, I think of something. "Hey, I would've taken your prizes if you didn't want them," I say.

Smack, thud. Walk, walk. The kid looks at me and shakes his head. "You've got to win your own," he says.

"You could've had, like, half that rack of stuffed animals over there," I say.

"What do I want with some worthless stuffed animals?"

"No, I know," I say, feeling stupid. "I didn't want those. I meant the cooler prizes, like those rubber basketballs."

"Cheap," says the kid.

"Could give 'em to a girlfriend or something, though," I say.

"You trying to give me love advice?" says the kid.

"I don't know," I say.

Smack, thud. Walk, walk. "You want to make yourself useful?"

"Sure," I say, springing to my feet.

"Go get the ball and pass it to me after I make it."

"Okay!"

He shoots it—*smack, thud.* I pick it up, and it looks

like it's from about 1901. The leather is brown and all slippery and worn away except for one part where it's peeling off. "Where'd you get this thing, World War Two?" I say, laughing at my own joke.

"Be quiet and pass it," says the kid. "I don't like to talk while I shoot."

He shoots. *Smack, thud.* He does this forever, and we don't say anything. Only two or three times does the ball hit the rim. The rest of the time, it goes straight through.

After about a half hour, I say, "So what's your name?"

"Jimmy."

He just keeps shooting, moving around here and there occasionally, and I keep passing until my arms hurt. I could really go for a hamburger or something, so to avoid thinking about my hunger, I pretend I'm giving Jimmy passes in real games, and he's scoring every time. The fans are cheering. The scoreboard numbers are going up, up, up. We're killing the other team. I'm the best passer there is, and Jimmy's the best shooter. Trying to fire up the crowd, I go for a behind-the-back pass. The ball flies off into the grass and Jimmy has to walk after it. When he gets to it and picks it up, he squints his eyes at me.

He swears and says, "Showboating's for girls."

"Sorry," I say. I fetch and pass for another long while. Jimmy misses four shots that whole time.

Finally, I say, "I'm getting kind of tired."

"Wanna quit?" says Jimmy.

"Only if you do," I say.

"A hundred more," he says, and shoots a hundred more, missing only three. I count in my head, and I know he does, too, because he stops after the last one and kicks the ball out into some open grass where you can barely see it.

"I'm thirsty," he says. "Wanna go buy me a Gatorade?"

"Sure," I say. "What color?"

"Red," he says. He gives me a five-dollar bill.

I run back into the main part of the fair and go up to a concession stand and order a red Gatorade. The lady gives me some change, and I run the Gatorade to Jimmy. He's sitting with his back against the barn wall.

"Where's yours?" he says, taking the drink and the change.

"I didn't have any money," I say.

Jimmy cracks open his Gatorade and guzzles it. He's sweating a little, and he puts the bottle against his head. I watch him drink it all the way gone. He chucks the bottle out in the grass by the ball, and we just sit there, staring. The sun's starting to set, and I probably better get back. But I don't want to leave Jimmy.

"I'm hungry now," he says. "You?"

I'm starving, but I say, "Nah. I had a big lunch."

"Let's go get a couple corn dogs," he says. "I'll buy you one for the rebounding."

"All right," I say.

Jimmy buys himself three corn dogs and me one. He buys two red Gatorades and gives me one. We sit down on a bench and chow. It tastes so good.

"I see you're eating that thing sideways," says Jimmy. "What happened to your tooth?"

"Got in a fight," I say.

"Must've tangled with a tiger."

"Pretty much."

"Where you live?"

"With my Uncle Stretch." I take a long, delicious swig of Gatorade.

Jimmy looks up from his corn dogs for the first time. "No kidding? Your uncle is Stretch?"

"Yeah," I say. "But I don't like him that much. He's sort of a jerk."

"Stretch ain't a jerk," says Jimmy. "You know he played college football at the U of M, and some people said he could've made the pros?"

"No. How do you know that?"

"Everybody knows Stretch," says Jimmy. "My brother Jorry was good friends with Roland, Stretch's boy. They were killed in the same car crash."

"Really?" I say. "Weird."

Jimmy goes back to one of his corn dogs.

"Was Roland cool?"

"Yes," says Jimmy. "He and Jorry were both studs."

"How'd they crash their car?" I say.

"They were drinkin', probably," says Jimmy. "Nobody found out for sure. They rolled it and went in a ditch. It had just rained and the ditch was full up with rainwater. They were trapped in the vehicle, and it had landed flip-turned upside down. They didn't die from the crash, but from drownin' in the rainwater."

"Ew."

"Ew? That's what you got to say to that story?"

I shrug my shoulders. I don't know what else to say.

"What's your name, kid?" asks Jimmy.

"Percy."

"What?"

"Percy. My full name is Perseus. Named after the Greek warrior."

"That's weird. You're an oddball, kid."

I shrug again.

"I gotta get goin'," says Jimmy. He clears his last corn dog off its stick with a big bite, gets up, and walks away. I'd like to follow this guy around some more, but he probably wouldn't be too cool with that. I look around and wander off. I can go wherever I want.

Chapter 16
PENNY CONSIDERS WOMANHOOD

Dear Mom,

I would like to officially report to you that I am now a woman, even though I am still a couple of weeks from my thirteenth birthday. As fate would have it, all of us were watching the adult talent show (I got fourth prize for my presentation on African sleeping sickness in the youth talent show) at the county fair when it happened. I was sitting with Sheryl and June Bug, and just a few rows away was this boy Wesley, whom I met in the horse barn a couple of days ago. Wesley is supernice, and has the most amazing horse ever, this black stallion named Mick.

For some dumb reason (that reason being that June Bug loaned them to me and told me how cute I looked), I chose to wear white shorts that day, and Sheryl was the one to notice when we stood up to clap for this really old farmer who was doing a yodeling thing. I got my predicament publicly announced by Sheryl (whose voice could carry through peat-bog mud, I swear) when she yelled out, "Oh, honey! You've started your period." Her voice bounced off the metal machine shed and probably carried into the next barns, so that all the kids showing cattle, horses, ducks, geese, rabbits, and canned goods were duly informed, as well. She wrapped her sweatshirt around my waist (I'm sure she was more than happy to take it off and display her low-cut tank top!) and hustled me off to the ladies' room. I was too mortified to look over to see Wesley's reaction. I was so ashamed. It was horrid.

To be honest, I didn't react very well. I started breathing really fast and nearly fainted. Sheryl's never said anything mean to me before, but at that moment, she grabbed my arm hard and told me to snap out of it, which I did fairly quickly.

Right there, before we were anywhere near the bathroom, she pulled out supplies and told me to go and clean myself up. When I came back out of the bathroom, she was waiting for me. She dug around in her purse for a while (Her purse has an enormous unicorn head on it and is the size of a normal person's suitcase, so you can imagine what a production it is for her to find anything in there. One time I saw her produce a pair of Rollerblades, a helmet, and knee pads for Pauly out of that thing!) and finally pulled out a bottle of Midol. She tapped out two pills and gave me a drink of her Dr Pepper. Then we sat on a curb outside the 4-H building for a while. She smoked a cigarette (right in my face!) and rubbed my back and told me to relax. Then she asked me how it felt to be officially a woman. I felt better then, because I did feel kind of special even if it was really embarrassing for a little bit.

When we joined the rest of the family, Sheryl told everyone to leave me alone and be nice and not say or do one annoying thing toward me. The strange thing is that they all listened. They sort of looked at me as a person to be feared or respected. June Bug was very concerned for me, but I couldn't tell if it was real concern, fake concern, or just masked jealousy. She may know more about horses and chickens, but I think it's obvious to her now that I'm the more mature one.

Do you think my breasts will blossom now?

You probably would like to hear some more about Wesley. Wesley Calvin Richter goes to the school we're going to attend if you have to stay in jail and can't come and get us off this farm. He's so nice. He's a whiz with animals. He's also really good with computers and technology, and he told me he could help me with my homework whenever I wanted once school starts. I told him thanks, and I didn't mention that I probably wouldn't need help because I didn't want to hurt his feelings. He's really gentle with his horse, Mick (short for Michelob, he said, but don't worry, because Wesley said he's not a drinker). He doesn't mind sending me things in the regular snail mail, due to the fact that Stretch's farm is in some sort of technological black hole and doesn't get cell phone reception or Internet. I know he's older than me, but I don't think it's a big deal because I'm so mature for my age and will probably always end up attracting older guys because of that.

Stretch said that Wesley is a good kid, whose dad used to play football with Stretch back in the day. His dad's name is Willy, and Stretch said that you'd remember him because he used to pester you about going out constantly when you all were in high school a million years ago.

I hope you're not considering going on a date with Wesley's dad. I have a number of good reasons.

1. That'd be weird because I like his son. And mothers and daughters should not date men from the same family.
2. The relationships of young people should take precedence over the relationships of old people,

because old people have already had their chances to have romantic relationships and messed them up.

3. It's way too soon after the divorce for you to start dating. I wouldn't mind if you went on a date in like a year or two maybe, but not yet. I mean, you just wrecked one nuclear family, and I think you need a break.

4. You'll be very busy finding a place for all of us to live once you get out (*if* you get out) and won't have time to date.

5. I really, really like Wesley and don't want you hanging around all the time embarrassing me with all your talk about the poor and health care and service to the community. I like all that stuff, too, Mom, but sometimes you do go on and on.

Maybe you need to lighten up a little bit. One thing I would recommend is looking into the eye of a horse. That seems to put everything in perspective for me.

Well, that's the update. Hope things are going okay in jail.

Love,
Penny

Dear Diary,
I've been in my room for three straight days, which

apparently is Pauly's threshold for giving me peace and quiet. All day long, he's been coming up to my bedroom door and peeking in the keyhole. Sometimes he sits down out there and sticks his little brown fingers underneath the door. A couple of times, Sheryl has hollered at him to scat, and he has. But he always comes back up the stairs, clomping like a maniac in his cowboy boots.

I know he's just curious about what I'm doing in here, but the truth is I'm not quite sure myself. I've put myself into a kind of self-imposed exile, like the Dalai Lama or something. I just want to be alone. I want to clear my head. I want to lie here, folded over this pillow, and rest. Sheryl brought me a heating pad, some bubble bath, an outdated *People* magazine with Angelina Jolie on the cover with about a thousand babies and apparently expecting two more (who do these people who have four, five, six kids think they are? Don't they know that the earth's already overcrowded?), and two extra-strength Midols.

My brain's firing away with all sorts of random thoughts. Things I'd forgotten, like science lessons and social studies homework from two years ago, are coming back to me and making more sense. I'm remembering Mom sitting all three of us kids at the little tables in all of our different homes to teach us math or taking us on nature walks or to science and art museums or to look at star constellations. I think Mom was a really good teacher. I wonder if she could become a real teacher once she gets out, since her nursing license has been revoked. I'm thinking a lot about Dad and Mom and God and religion.

I remember studying entrainment, which is the synchronization of rhythms. For instance, a roomful of grandfather clocks will coordinate the swing of their pendulums, no matter how unevenly they may have begun swinging. Fireflies trapped in a glass will coordinate their flashing. I remember studying vocabulary words, too. *Taboo*, a word often associated with discussion about womanly things, actually gets its origin from the Polynesian culture and their word *tapua*, which means "sacred."

Then I started thinking about Dad. I wonder if he's missing us or if he's happy to be rid of us. I think about all his sermons on women's and men's and children's roles in the family. I think he was probably right about a lot of things, like being nice and sharing with the poor, but he was misguided about a lot of other things, like men being the head of the household. I think Dad is flawed, which is okay. I guess all humans are. But I'm having a hard time figuring out if he was always flawed and I just didn't notice or if he became flawed suddenly because Mom drove him to it. Or did he become flawed suddenly all on his own or because of something I did wrong? I worry sometimes that I drove my parents to make bad mistakes. I wonder if I could have been a better daughter. I worry that my parents wish they had never had me. Maybe they think having us kids was a big mistake. I worry that I or my brothers ruined my parents' lives.

I thought about talking to June Bug about all this stuff because she might understand how I feel, especially since she was practically conceived at a rock concert by two people who didn't even know each other that well. I decided not to, though.

Last night, I snuck downstairs and took a cigarette and lighter out of Sheryl's purse. I'm not sure why I did that exactly, but I think it has to do with accepting flaws. I know it's a bad flaw to smoke, but having that flaw doesn't make the smoker a bad person. I just wanted to see what smoking felt like and why people do it. So I went upstairs to the attic and lit up the cigarette. I put it to my lips and tried to breathe like I'd seen Sheryl do. The cigarette tasted like rotten coffee and tea all mixed together with dirty horse feed and nail polish remover, so I stopped. But I think a little of the smoke went into my lungs because I got this weird, calm feeling. The attic was really hot and flooded with eerie moonlight coming through the tiny window. I didn't smoke the cigarette anymore, but I let it burn. The only moving particles in the attic were the floating dust specks and the curling smoke off the red ember as it burned down to the filter. I snuffed it onto the floor and made sure it was completely out. I spit on the butt and kicked it aside.

I didn't dare turn on any lights because Percy would have seen it from his granary room and come to investigate. All around me were trunks and boxes of stuff, but I didn't open them. The attic wasn't bright enough to see very well, and some of the boxes didn't have tops. I could see into them without snooping. Mostly, they were full of regular things like old baby blankets, sleeping bags, some toys like trucks and a train set, someone's old football uniform, a pile of women's Levi's jeans and cowboy boots. All the stuff told me that Stretch once had a regular nuclear family, too, and that his nuclear family disintegrated just like mine.

Maybe it's just none of my business what happened to it. Maybe he'll tell me when he's ready, or maybe it's okay to leave some things in the past.

Today, outside, Percy and June Bug are spraying down the horses with the hose. Even the mean one. Pauly's back. He's sliding a piece of paper under my door with a drawing of a big, black, stick-legged horse on it. He's sweet. I may be ready to come out of my room now.

Dear Dad,

You might be interested to know that I am a woman now and have a different, more mature perspective of many things.

How's the new church looking? How's the new accountant working out? Is she good with numbers?

I am pretty disappointed in you, Dad. But it's probably not entirely your fault. I may not have previously noticed that you have flaws like all other human beings. I may have looked past them. But since I've become a woman, I see things a lot more clearly. I can see that Mom had some really good points about your being a hypocrite. When I think about all those sermons and men's conferences you gave about the Family First! movement and then compare those words to how you've abandoned and ignored Percy, Pauly, and me, I get really, really disappointed in you. But you are my father no matter what, so I still love you.

Penny

DEAR OKONKWO,

HOW IS EVERYTHING IN AFRICA? LIFE'S PRETTY HECTIC HERE, BUT I STILL FIND TIME TO WRITE YOU. I THINK YOU SHOULD TAKE MORE CARE TO RESPOND TO MY LETTERS. I UNDERSTAND YOU ARE PROBABLY PRETTY BUSY,

TOO, BUT ONE OF THE REASONS I AGREED TO
SEND MONEY TO YOU WAS BECAUSE I THOUGHT
I WOULD RECEIVE REGULAR UPDATES FROM MY
ADOPTED CHILD. I THINK IT WOULD SHOW
SOME MATURITY AND GRATITUDE ON YOUR
PART TO WRITE MORE REGULARLY TO ME SO
THAT I WOULD FEEL LIKE I'M GETTING
SOMETHING OUT OF SPONSORING YOU. RIGHT
NOW IT FEELS LIKE A ONE-SIDED
RELATIONSHIP WITH ME GIVING EVERYTHING
AND YOU TAKING EVERYTHING.

MAYBE THAT'S HOW THINGS WORK IN YOUR
WORLD. MAYBE IT'S NOT YOUR FAULT YOU'RE
BEING SO SELFISH AND YOU CAN'T EVEN HELP
IT. MAYBE NO ONE EVER TAUGHT YOU HOW TO
BE POLITE. I KNOW YOU PROBABLY DON'T
KNOW MUCH ABOUT CHRISTIANITY BECAUSE
YOU PROBABLY PRACTICE SOME OTHER KIND OF
RELIGION, BUT SOME PEOPLE DON'T EVEN NEED
TO KNOW ONE THING ABOUT ANY RELIGION TO
BE NICE AND HAVE MANNERS. THERE ARE SOME
PEOPLE IN THE WORLD WHO DON'T BELIEVE IN
JESUS WHO DO LOTS OF GREAT WORKS. THERE'S
THIS GUY NAMED GANDHI, FOR INSTANCE, WHO
LAY AROUND WITH THE POOR AND
UNTOUCHABLE PEOPLE IN INDIA ALL DAY, NEVER
EVEN WORRYING ONE BIT ABOUT HOW DIRTY

AND FULL OF GERMS THEY WERE. THERE IS THIS OTHER GUY, TOO, CALLED THE DALAI LAMA, WHO JUST SITS AND MEDITATES FOR THE FREEDOM OF A WHOLE COUNTRY CALLED TIBET. THOSE TWO GUYS DON'T KNOW ANYTHING ABOUT JESUS, BUT THEY STILL CARE ABOUT THEIR FELLOW MAN. YOU SHOULD THINK LONG AND HARD ABOUT THAT, OKONKWO.

SINCERELY,
PENELOPE PRIBYL

Chapter 17

Percy, Pauly, and Lightning

WHEN WE get home from the pool, a few days after the fair is over, Sheryl has dinner all laid out on the table. It's some kind of hot dish with a lot of potatoes in it, salad, corn on the cob, and watermelon. I am hungry and sit right down to eat.

"Wash your hands," says Uncle Stretch.

"But they're not even dirty," I say.

"Get to the bathroom and wash up," says Uncle Stretch, giving me the eye.

"But I've been at the pool! I've had water on them all day!"

Uncle Stretch gets up from his chair and reaches out. *Whap!* I get one on the side of the head. It stings, so I yelp and hold my head with both hands.

"Oh, just go already," says Penny.

"Yeah," says Pauly. "Ev-we-one knows it didn't hoht that bad."

I want to tell Pauly to shut up, but Uncle Stretch is standing too close. I go into the bathroom to wash my hands. They don't know it, but I don't even use soap.

Back at the table, Pauly's bragging to everyone about how he was doing all these cool jumps off the diving board and how one of the lifeguards told him it was so great. I saw it myself, and believe me, Pauly's jumps off the diving board are *not* anything to brag about. It's like he runs slowly off the board with his hands straight out like a mummy's and then his feet keep running until he hits the water. No dives, no cannonballs, no can openers, no jackknives, no belly busters, no preachers, no flips, nothing. Mummy hands and running feet—every single time. But I decide to let him brag because I know everyone will just yell at me if I tell the truth.

I wait for him to quit bragging and then sit there while June Bug tells how she met this new girl who moved to town who's going to be in the same grade as her. She blabs how they played freeze tag all after-noon and then when it was break time, they shared a Cherry Coke. Whoop-de-doo!

Then it's Penny's turn to bore us. I had gotten kind of used to her hanging out in her room, which she did for about three days, but ever since she's come out of there, she's been trying to act older than she is or something. She starts telling everyone about this boring book she was reading the whole time at the pool. Something about Eleanor of Aquitaine and medieval castles and treason and blah, blah, blah, blah, blah.

I can barely take it anymore. "Penny never even got her hair wet," I say. "She just sat there reading and applying and reapplying sunscreen to make sure she didn't get skin cancer. What a waste!"

Everyone looks at me like I farted or something.

"What!" I say.

"You're a jerk, that's what," says June Bug.

"Sherylynn," says her mother.

"Naw, she's right," says Uncle Stretch. "Girl's calling a spade a spade, is all."

Whatever that means! Nobody says anything for a couple of minutes. All you can hear is people using their forks or chewing, mostly Pauly, because he's a big hog at the dinner table. I look over at Penny, who usually has some sympathy on her face for people who get called names, but she just glares back at me for a couple of seconds and then slowly continues eating.

Then Sheryl breaks the silence. "Well, Percy, what did you do at the pool today?"

"Nothing," I say.

"You better have something to say for yourself if you're going to shoot down your sister's story, buddy," says Uncle Stretch. His dinner fork and knife are raised about his plate like he's going to slash me to bits if I don't talk.

"Well," I say, mumbling, "I just swam around and went off the board a few times, like Pauly, except, you know, like real jumps and stuff . . ." I look at everybody's faces, and they don't look very supportive of my telling the truth. I keep talking, anyway. "And then at break, I went outside the fence to talk to this teenager kid, Jimmy, who was shooting hoops by himself. I thought maybe he'd like some company or something, so I rebounded for him for a while. A long time, actually, because I missed the whole next swim period. When Jimmy is shooting, and I'm rebounding, I kind of lose track of time. It's like Jimmy making the shot and me getting the ball and making a perfect pass to him is all that matters. So . . . that's what I did."

"Jimmy Fredrichs?" says Uncle Stretch.

"I don't know his last name," I say.

"Is this the first time you met this boy?" asks Sheryl.

"No," I say. "I met him at the fair. He was shooting baskets, and I rebounded for him there, too. He makes pretty much every shot."

"Dark hair?" asks Uncle Stretch. "Kinda skinny, dresses like a hooligan? Doesn't talk much?"

"Yeah, he barely says a word," I say. "Although I think he looks pretty cool, actually."

"That's Jimmy Fredrichs."

"He told me some stuff about your son," I say.

Penny's head snaps up from her plate.

"His brother Jorry was a good friend of Roland's," says Uncle Stretch.

I say, "Jimmy told me his brother and Roland died in the same car crash."

Pretty much everybody has stopped eating by now. Penny, in particular, sits there with her mouth open—and not because she's about to take a bite of her food. Sheryl puts her hand on Uncle Stretch's shoulder and rubs it.

Uncle Stretch looks at me. Then he looks at Sheryl, like he's only talking to her. "Jimmy's got a good heart, but he's a punk, got some dumb ideas," he says. "Smokes and drinks. Could be the best basketball player in school but doesn't even go out for the team."

"Why not?" I ask.

Uncle Stretch turns back to me. "Why don't you ask him?" he says. "You two are thick as thieves, sounds like."

"I don't even know where he lives," I say. "I've just seen him around a couple times."

Uncle Stretch snorts. "If you paid attention to more than just yourself, you'd've probably realized by now that Jimmy lives right up the road," he says. "'Bout two miles north."

I can see this conversation has gotten underneath Uncle Stretch's skin, so I just ask for another piece of corn. June Bug passes me the plate, and I take an ear and start in. Nobody's saying anything again, so I try to lighten things up.

"So who gets to drive me up to the state fair this weekend?" I ask. "Did you figure it out?"

Uncle Stretch looks at Sheryl. Sheryl looks at Uncle Stretch. Uncle Stretch picks up a piece of watermelon and takes a bite.

"We were just discussing that, hon," says Sheryl, "and it's a dilemma. Stretch has to load and deliver hogs the day you're supposed to be in the fair, and I've got a baby shower I planned on throwing for my sister two months ago."

Uncle Stretch spits a watermelon seed onto his plate and says, "Doesn't look good."

"You don't even have a new chicken picked out, ee-thoh," says Pauly.

"Shut up, Pauly," I say.

"Don't talk to him like that," says Penny.

"Pauly's got a point," says Uncle Stretch. "Have you given one second to getting a new chicken ready? There's not much use in taking you up there if you're not prepared."

"I'm prepared!" I say. "I chose a new one. I just need to clean him up. June Bug said she'd help."

June Bug rolls her eyes. "Maybe your fake girl-friend, Elle, can help you with your chicken, and maybe she can give you a ride to the state fair, too."

My face goes red. "What are you even talking about?" I say.

"Pauly and I saw you talking to that picture on the wall in the granary. We heard you calling her Elle and being all mushy with her."

Penny's eyes widen. "I *knew* he was doing dirty things in there!" she says.

"All that proves is that you were spying on me," I say. "And as for anything else, I don't even know what you're talking about!" I back up my chair and ask to be excused.

"Sherylynn!" says her mom. "Apologize!"

"No!" says June Bug.

Now it's Sheryl's turn to blush.

"Now wait a cotton-pickin' minute," says Uncle Stretch. He lays his silverware down, takes a deep breath, and exhales. "You won an entry in the state fair. We'll see what we can do to get you there. I might find somebody else to take you up. Let us think about it."

The idea strikes me like lightning. "What about Jimmy?" I say.

"Is he old enough to drive?" asks Sheryl.

"He said he was sixteen. I bet he'd do it," I say.

Uncle Stretch scratches his cheek. He says, "He may be busy himself."

"Well, can I at least ask?" I say.

Uncle Stretch sighs and says, "Sure."

"We can find his number in the phone book after dinner," says Sheryl.

"It's 445-3204," says Uncle Stretch.

"I think I'd rather run over there," I say, thinking it'd be cool to see where Jimmy lives. "I need a work-out. Which way is it from here?"

"Two and a half miles north," says Uncle Stretch. "Place with a crumbled silo and a big barn that's black instead of red, thanks to Jimmy painting it when he was in his gothic stage, or whatever they call it."

"So at the end of our driveway," I say, "I turn to the . . . ?"

"North," says Uncle Stretch.

"So that means I go to the left or . . . ?"

"Other left," says Uncle Stretch.

"Huh?" I say.

"Turn right, sweetie," says Sheryl.

We're on the gravel road after supper. I have to jog slower than usual to wait up for Pauly, who's riding his little dirt bike beside me. He rides annoyingly slow. Uncle Stretch and Sheryl made me bring him along because they said we need to learn how to get along better as brothers. I told them I was going to be running too fast for Pauly, doing a cardio workout, but they wouldn't have it. We've gone about a mile, but it's taken us forever. And the sky is getting dark.

"Jeez, Pauly!" I say. "Pick it up. It's going to rain on us."

"My foot hohts," says Pauly. "I stepped on a piece of glass at the pool, and it hohts to pwess the pedal."

"Whatever," I say. "Suck it up." I pick up the pace and run a little faster. He'll catch up. I can't wait to get to Jimmy's. The idea of taking a road trip with him—getting out of this stupid place for a while—sounds great to me. We would get a couple Gatorades on the drive up. Maybe Uncle Stretch would give us some money for a hotel, and we could go swimming, play some video games, maybe find a hoop and let Jimmy practice for a few hours. I would rebound a thousand shots. Jimmy would make nine hundred and ninety-nine. My new chicken would win the grand prize, and I'd win some money we could spend on pizza or more video games or . . . whatever we wanted. I realize, with all the good thoughts I'm having, I'm sprinting. I look back and see Pauly *way* behind. I stop.

"Pauly!" I yell. "Come on!"

I yell again, as loud as I can. Just then I feel a raindrop. I look up the road. We're about halfway to Jimmy's house. It's just as close for me to run that way as it is to head back to Uncle Stretch's. But then I see Pauly sitting down on the side of the road, his bike on its side. If I don't go back and get him, Uncle Stretch won't let me go to the state fair.

I start walking back to Pauly.

A huge lightning bolt juts across the sky, and thunder booms. I start to run. The rain picks up.

When I get to Pauly, I find him pouting, with his head down.

"What's wrong with you?" I say. "Dang it, Pauly, why do you have to mess everything up?"

"My foot," he says, and points to it.

Through his sandal, I can see dirt and some small pieces of gravel. And there's blood.

"Your foot's bleeding," I say.

The rain is really coming down now. It's hard to tell what's rain and what's tears on Pauly's face. He barely ever cries.

"C'mon, get up, Pauly."

He gets up, and I take his arm, and he limps a couple of steps. I try to get him to get going on his bike, but it's not working well. The lightning and thunder crackle, and the rain pours down. I felt less wet at the swimming pool!

"C'mon Pauly! We're going to get struck by lightning."

"I can't, Pohcy!" he says. "My foot hohts too much!"

He tugs away from me and falls to the ground and starts crying for sure. His mouth is wide open, and you can see all his teeth. What do I do? If I leave him in the ditch while I run back to Uncle Stretch's, he could get struck by lightning or hit by a car. I get an idea.

"Get on my back," I say. Pauly just lies there, bawling in the rain and thunder.

"Stand up!" I scream at him. I chuck his bike into the ditch, yank him to his feet, and then hoist him onto my back. He's heavy. But I start running back to Uncle Stretch's house. We both might get hit by lightning, but at least I'm trying to save us. Pauly's blubbering mouth is right next to my ear, and I can hear every sob.

"Ease up on the crying!" I yell. He doesn't. So I twirl in circles and make little bunny hops. He stops crying and says, "What ow you doing, dude?"

"Nothing," I say. I keep running and twirling, zigzagging and hopping. I almost fall a couple of times, but I don't. Pauly knows it's more of a game now, and he starts laughing. The rain is soaking us, the sky is blinking, and we're dashing for home.

Chapter 18

Penny, Future Medical Professional

Dear Diary,

Just when I thought I was getting things about my family figured out, I get a letter from my father that gets me all screwed up again. He tells me that their new church is complete. He tells me that he and Peggy are eager for us to join them in their new ministry. He says he'll be coming soon to pick us up. The letter is signed "Father and Mama Peg." *Mama Peg?!*

On the one hand, I think, *Who does he think he is? He basically abandoned us and abandoned Mom when we all needed his support the most!* On the other hand, I think, *This is our father. Fathers deserve respect and honor. This is the one who has prayed with us and provided for us all these years.* Maybe I just don't fully understand the circumstances of the past few months. Maybe our best chance for a nuclear family would be with him and Peggy? At least there'd be a mom and a dad.

But then I think about Mom. And I think about Stretch and Sheryl and even June Bug. Maybe sending us to Stretch *really* was for our own good. After all, don't I kind of like it here? Don't I kind of wish I could stay here? So then another part of me thinks, *Why is Father coming to get us now?* I wish I could be more like Percy and Pauly. They're so simple. When I read the letter to them, Pauly told me that he wanted to stay with Stretch. Percy said, "Write him back. Tell him I'm the pastor of the chicken coop and can't leave my flock." That Percy. He's funny sometimes.

Here is a letter I would like to send to "Mama Peg" (but probably won't):

Dear "Mama Peg,"

You're not my mother. You look fat in your bikini. I'm never, ever going to be nice to you so don't even dream about it.

Sincerely,

Penny

Besides the attic, I've found another place where I

can be alone. If I climb to the top of the old windmill, I can see for miles. I've also discovered that from up there, I can pick up cell phone reception! Wesley's been texting me sometimes. Occasionally, I sit there calmly looking out as far as Wesley's farm and the pasture where Mick runs around galloping like a normal horse should. I can't help but compare Mick to Brenda and Bernie, who just stand around all day looking mad about the quality of their lives.

I can just imagine a conversation between them:

Brenda: (Swishing her tail like mad and biting at a horsefly.) Bernie, I'm sick and tired of this place. I've been thinking of making a break for it. Just jumping this fence and galloping away forever.

Bernie: (Letting a whole swarm of horseflies bother him all they want.) Well, it's been a long while since I galloped. A long, long while.

Brenda: (Chomping teeth at nothing.) Can anyone blame me for being the crabbiest horse ever? This place is a real Horse Camp, all right?

Bernie: (Yawning.) A Horse Camp, indeed.

Brenda: I'm going to go over and bite the fence awhile. Don't mind me.

Bernie: I'm thinking nap. I'll see you when I wake up. If I'm still alive.

Dear Father,

The weather forecast looks ominous for the next ten days. Thunder and lightning with the chance of high winds and hail are on the way. There might even be a tornado. I think you'd better hold off until later in the month. Besides, there are some bumpy stretches in the gravel road to Stretch's house. Also, Percy's got to take his chickens to the state fair this weekend. Basically, this is just not that great a time for you to come for us. Busy, busy, busy! I'll drop you a note when things slow down around here.

Penelope

Dear Mom,

How are things in prison? Things here are all right.

I've made some decisions about my life. While I used to want to get married to a man who had a ministry like Dad and be the pretty wife who sat in the front or played the piano and sang and shuffled my kids up to the stage to sing a nice Christmas song in their cute little outfits, now I don't want to do that anymore. After my success at the county fair with my PowerPoint presentation on African sleeping sickness, I think I'll be a doctor or nurse, like you. Not the kind who gets arrested and goes to prison and disintegrates her nuclear family, but the kind who actually works in a hospital or travels to different countries telling the people there how to keep their kids healthy.

One thing I'll have to do so that I won't be a huge hypocrite is never to smoke again. Yes. I smoked a cigarette. I just really felt like doing it, and so I did. Let that be the extent of my teenaged rebellion. And even though I'm really confused about religion, I still think it's healthy to make a confession, so this is my confession. As you probably already know, Sheryl smokes like an exhaust pipe, and I borrowed a cigarette from her secret stash. I guess since I didn't ask her if I could have one, you could say that I stole it. I'd better confess that, too. Stealing, even outside the realm of religion, isn't a very moral thing to do. Anyway, after I tell her I'm sorry for stealing a cigarette, I'm going to make it my personal mission, as a future medical professional, to help Sheryl stop smoking. She's going to be my first patient. Isn't that a great idea?

Well, that's about all, besides the fact that Father says he's coming to pick us up and take us back home to live with him and "Mama Peg." Um, Mama Peg?

I wish you'd write to him and give him a piece of your mind. Doesn't it bother you that he's trying to replace you so quickly with some hoochie mama in a bikini? Anyway, this really isn't a good time for us to be leaving, what with my helping Sheryl quit smoking and Percy's state fair chicken show coming up. Please pass along the message to Father.

Love and kisses,
Penny

DEAR OKONKWO,

THOUGH MY LETTER TO YOU IS RIGHT ON SCHEDULE, IT FEELS AS THOUGH I HAVE NOT WRITTEN IN A LONG TIME. LIFE IN AMERICA IS VERY, VERY BUSY. HOW ARE YOUR ENGLISH STUDIES COMING ALONG?

I HOPE YOU ARE SAVING SOME OF MY MONTHLY DONATIONS TO BUY BOOKS SO THAT YOU CAN LEARN AND BETTER YOUR CIRCUMSTANCES. YOU DON'T WANT TO BE LIVING IN A STRAW HUT YOUR WHOLE LIFE, SO YOU HAVE TO SAVE SOME MONEY, BUY ENGLISH BOOKS, GET EDUCATED, AND BUY A NEW HOUSE MADE OF WOOD OR MAYBE EVEN BRICK. I LIVED IN A NICE BRICK HOUSE ONCE, AND IT WAS QUITE LOVELY, IF A LITTLE COLD IN THE WINTERTIME. NOT THAT YOU'D WORRY ABOUT THE COLD IN NIGERIA.

ANYWAY, I WAS THRILLED TO RECEIVE YOUR LETTER AND SORRY TO HEAR ABOUT HOW YOUR

DOG RAN OFF WITH A PACK OF WILD DOGS AND
NEVER CAME BACK. NEXT TIME YOU GET A DOG
(WHY NOT JUST GO OUT AND TRAP A DIFFERENT
WILD DOG?) YOU BETTER TIE HIM UP AT NIGHT
AND GIVE HIM PLENTY OF FOOD AND WATER SO
THAT HE DOESN'T HAVE TO GO LOOKING FOR
THEM ELSEWHERE.

ALSO, IT IS WONDERFUL NEWS THAT YOUR
FATHER INVITED A NICE AMERICAN LADY TO
YOUR HUT TO VISIT. AND IT CERTAINLY *IS*
INTERESTING THE WAY HE CREATES "AUTHENTIC"
MARRIAGE CEREMONY EXPERIENCES FOR A
"VERY AFFORDABLE" PRICE. IT SOUNDS LIKE A
GREAT EXPERIENCE FOR LONELY FEMALE
TOURISTS TO NIGERIA. I AM SORRY, BUT I CAN'T
THINK OF ANYONE WHO MIGHT BE INTERESTED
IN SUCH AN EXPERIENCE. YOUR DAD MUST BE A
VERY CLEVER MAN! SO WILL THIS WOMAN BE
YOUR STEPMOTHER NOW? BECAUSE IF SO, I CAN
TELL YOU ALL ABOUT HAVING TO DEAL WITH
MIXED FAMILIES AND ALL.

LIFE HERE HAS BEEN BUSY. I'M SURE YOU
HAVE NO IDEA, AS LIFE IN AFRICA SEEMS TO
GO MUCH SLOWER AND EASIER THAN HERE. I
WON'T GET INTO ALL THE DETAILS, BUT I'VE
BEEN VERY HARD AT WORK HERE ON MY UNCLE'S
FARM AND HAVE BEEN SPENDING A LOT OF TIME

THINKING ABOUT MY FUTURE CAREER.
  WELL, THAT'S ALL FOR NOW, OKONKWO!
  SINCERELY, YOUR FRIEND,
  PENELOPE

P.S. YES, NOW THAT I'VE HAD SOME TIME TO REFLECT, I CAN SEE THAT MY LAST LETTER MAY HAVE BEEN OVERLY CRITICAL OF YOU, ESPECIALLY SINCE I NOW KNOW ABOUT THE TERRIBLE GOVERNMENT CORRUPTION, THE FAMINE, AND THE OTHER HARD TIMES YOU ARE EXPERIENCING. YOU ARE RIGHT ABOUT MY NOT BEING THE ONLY PERSON IN THE WORLD WITH TROUBLES, AND I AM SORRY THAT I ASSUMED YOU DIDN'T KNOW ANYTHING ABOUT GANDHI OR THE DALAI LAMA WHEN YOU OBVIOUSLY DO KNOW QUITE A BIT ALREADY.

Note to Sheryl:
  Now that you have moved in and are around night and day, I feel I am obligated to inform you of your death sentence. I'm worried about your health. I'm not sure anyone has told you, but smoking makes you smell bad.
  Breathing secondhand smoke can kill your loved ones.

Smoking gives you wrinkles, especially ones around your mouth. Ew.

Smokers get way more cavities in their teeth than regular people.

Smokers cough all the time, and other people think they're always contagious and tend to avoid them. I'm going to be a nurse when I grow up, and I'm very concerned about your well-being.

Text Message to Wesley:

Thx 4 wrtg bck. U shld try 2 ride Mick ovr 2mrrw so we can hng out n lstn 2 this cd u mad 4 me. Cn't w8.

Chapter 19
Percy Celebrates His Birthday

I WAKE UP a little earlier than normal. The alarm clock says 7:32. I sing "Happy Birthday" to myself, because that's a tradition I started a few years back. Ah . . . thirteen years old, an official teenager! The sun shines into the granary, reflecting off the Joe Montana poster, off Tommy Kramer, off the very lifelike Adrian Peterson picture I recently drew and hung. Birds are chirping outside. I run my tongue over my missing tooth and it doesn't bother me—it even feels less jagged than usual. I feel the faint line of my chin scar. I'm hoping it doesn't entirely disappear. I get up out of bed and stretch in the sunbeams coming in the window. I go over to Elle and tell her she's looking especially beautiful today and give her a little kiss on the cheek. Birthdays are great.

I put on my old Vikings sweatshirt and my favorite pair of blue jeans. I decide to start my birthday with my favorite person: Elle. For about an hour, I gaze at her loveliness and draw her into my sketch pad. I draw her in different poses. In one, she drops the arm covering her breast.

When I've done as many drawings of Elle as I feel like, I decide to go into the house, even though it's still early, to see who's wrapped up some presents for me. On my way through the yard, I can hear Uncle Stretch shoveling something in the barn. As I walk past the barn doorway, the shoveling stops, and Uncle Stretch pokes his head out. I smile at him and get ready for the first person of the day to say happy birthday to me.

"After breakfast, why don't you come out and power-wash the chicken coop," he says.

"Uh, *okay*," I say, annoyed.

He looks at me hard. "You got some kind of problem with doing your chores?"

"No," I say, and keep walking toward the house. What's the deal? Is no day sacred around here?

I decide to walk into the kitchen. Maybe Sheryl's got a birthday cake waiting. She's often up, rattling around the kitchen early, since she and June Bug officially moved in a couple of weeks ago. Though it's a little weird to have those two around full-time, it balances things out as far as having an equal number of males and females in the house, and I kind of like Sheryl doing Mom-like things in the kitchen or whatever. As for June Bug, sometimes she's cool, sometimes she's annoying. This morning, Sheryl's washing dishes, but there's no cake sitting out or anything, and all she says is, "Good morning, Percy," not "Happy birthday." I look at her like, *Aren't you forgetting something?* but I'm pretty sure she doesn't get it.

There's no birthday breakfast waiting, no pancakes or bacon or eggs, so I go into the cupboard and pull out the box of Cap'n Crunch. I shake it. It's empty. Who puts an empty box back in the cupboard? Pauly, for sure. There's no other good cereal—only Grape-Nuts, Raisin Bran, and Shredded Wheat. I go for Shredded Wheat. I pour some milk on it and choke down about a half of a wheat square thing before I decide it tastes too much like desert sand for me to continue eating it. I drink the milk out of the bowl— the milk that hasn't been sucked up already by the dry, old Shredded Wheat—and call it good. Some birthday breakfast.

I creep up the stairs and stick my head in Penny's room. It's her birthday, too! She's sleeping. I tiptoe down the hall. I look inside my old room and hear

Pauly snoring away on the bottom bunk and June Bug snoring away on the top bunk. Pauly's snoring is kind of high and light and June Bug's is kind of low. It almost sounds like a song or a harmony or something. Whatever. It's not that great or anything.

I decide to head out to the barn to see about my chores. Maybe Uncle Stretch was just joking about power-washing that chicken coop. Maybe he'll have a new four-wheeler ATV out there waiting for me with a big bow on top. That'd be pretty sweet.

When I get out to the barn, there's no four-wheeler. There's just Uncle Stretch, emptying big buckets of pig food into troughs. Pigs grunt and snort. The one that marked my chin for life with its hoof is in there somewhere. I have to clear my throat three times before Uncle Stretch turns around and notices me.

"Well, what are you waiting for?" he asks. "Go on into the chicken coop and get to power-washing." He turns around and continues shoveling.

I head for the doorway.

"Hey!" says Uncle Stretch.

"Yeah?" I say.

"You pick out your new chicken for the state fair?"

"Sort of, but not exactly."

"You ask Jimmy yet about taking you up to the Cities for the fair?"

"No," I say.

"What are you waiting for?"

"I don't know."

"The fair's in three days, you know."

"Yeah, it's this Friday."

"Your competition is on Saturday," says Uncle Stretch.

"Yeah, I know what day it is," I say, *do you?*

Uncle Stretch just gives me one of his bad looks and says, "Watch your stinkin' mouth," and turns around and starts shoveling again.

"Maybe I'll go over to ask Jimmy right now," I say.

Uncle Stretch turns around. "After power-washing," he says.

Power-washing the chicken coop is really disgusting. Definitely not a chore for doing on your birthday. First, I herd all the chickens out into the yard, and then I fire up the power washer. Those chickens crap everywhere, and I have to blow their mess away with the powerful streams of water. Sometimes bits of chicken crap get on your arms, or clothes, or face. Uncle Stretch says you're supposed to shovel any crap up when you're done, but I just keep blasting with the pressure washer until it's out the door or at least jammed up into a corner. Uncle Stretch says power-washing for too long wastes water, but who cares? The washer feels kind of like a gun in my hands, and I imagine I'm a soldier, blowing things away. I spray the walls and the ceiling for fun every once in a while.

While I'm power-washing, I think about birthdays in my past. On my ninth birthday, we were living out in Connecticut, and my grandparents—before they died—and some of my aunts, uncles, and cousins came to this big party my mom and dad threw for me, and we had this huge family football game. When I was eight, we celebrated my birthday in New Guinea, and we hiked to this natural waterfall where we had a really cool picnic, and I got a ton of presents, including this tiger-tooth necklace that some really poor kid gave to me, which I still sometimes wear to this day. When I was seven, we were in Africa, and my birthday fell on the same day the tribe we were staying with had this big rain celebration. There were all kinds of crazy food and games and music, and at the end of the day, there was a rain dance. My dad knew the tribal leader and I think he pulled some strings, because in the middle of the big rain dance that night, which was the highlight of the entire day, the tribal leader picked me and Penny to come up and dance in the middle of the rain circle. Only four lucky individuals get to dance in the middle of the rain circle each year, and we were two of them. Then, coolest of all, it rained, which meant the rain celebration worked.

I've always believed that my dancing helped it rain that day, or God or something made it rain because of my dance, which is pretty freaky and cool at the same time. One year we were in the Philippines and didn't get any presents, but, hey, at least Mom made a cake and I got to spend the whole day searching for Japanese gold.

I finish power-washing the chicken coop, and I do some general cleanup and look over the flock. I decide on a decent-looking creature I name Hercules II, who will be my new show chicken. I wash him up, clean him good, and this takes the rest of the morning. Before lunch, I walk down to the end of the driveway to check the mail, hoping for at least a few birthday cards. Only four pieces of mail: two junk letters for Uncle Stretch, a grocery ad, and a letter for Penny with *Mom* on the return address.

I hike upstairs and swing open the door to Penny's bedroom. She's got her nose in that weird Cowboy Zombie book she's been toting around, and when I barge in, she whips the book off her bed like she's ashamed of it. I raise an eyebrow. "Hey," I say. "Why don't you open this letter and see if Mom sent us anything, like money or whatever."

Penny looks up from her scriptures. "Why would she be sending us money?"

I look at her like, *Isn't it obvious?*

Penny opens the letter and reads it. It takes like two full minutes. "Here," she says, handing it to me. "You might as well read it for yourself, since it has some good advice that could pertain to both of us. And also, it wouldn't hurt you to pay some attention to what Mom's been doing in jail. You never even write her."

"Why don't you just tell me what it says?" I say.

Penny looks at me with a very non-Jesus-like look on her face. "No," she says. "Read it yourself. I will not be an enabler to your disengagement with our parents and their *situation*."

She says the word *situation* like it's a swear word. "I'm not reading it," I say. "So just tell me. There's no money in there?"

"No, Percy," says Penny, "there's no money in there." She shakes her head slowly at me like I'm a two-year-old kid, and I've accidentally gone potty in the bathtub or something. "Philippians 4:19 comes to mind," she adds. "Remember that verse, the one Dad used to recite in his sermons? 'God shall supply all your needs according to his riches in glory by Christ Jesus.' Did you get that? According to *his* riches. Not yours."

"He only recited that verse because he was passing around the money-collection plate."

"The point is," says Penny, "that you should stop being so greedy."

"All I'm looking for is a couple bucks," I say. "Riches is more than a couple bucks, don't you think?"

"I think you should try to figure that out for yourself," says Penny. "And I think that maybe you should stop turning your back on God and making *me* responsible for telling you that you're a huge sinner!"

"God's not saying that!" I yell. "You are!" I pick up the dumb novel she threw on the floor and place it gently on her bed. "And, by the way, these days you seem to be reading more of this Cowboy Zombie book than the Bible, which nobody really understands anyhow. It says things like, 'It's unclean to eat a rabbit' or 'Job praised the Lord after the Lord killed his whole family.' Do you think that really happened, Penny? Why would anyone praise the Lord for killing his family?"

"Blasphemy!" says Penny. Her face is all red and her hands are crunched into fists. I can tell she's about to start crying.

"You're a bigger sinner than I am," I say, even though I know I shouldn't. And then I say something else, just because I know it will mess her up. "You probably wonder yourself sometimes if God is even real."

"You're wrong!" screams Penny. "Remember this verse? Matthew 7:13. 'Enter through the narrow gate, for wide is the gate and broad is the road that leads to destruction!' Enter through the narrow gate, Percy, or you will be destroyed! Stay off the wide road!"

"Great!" I holler. "Thanks for the info." Then I think of something else to say. I smile and let it out: "Maybe you should stay out of the attic and stop smoking cigarettes."

Her face goes red—well, redder than it already is. "*What?*" she shrieks. "What are you talking about?"

"I know what you do up there at night with all the smoking. You're a bigger sinner than me. You're a giant Horse Camp."

"You don't know what you're talking about!" she screams.

"Penny, when you smoke, it smells like smoke," I say. "And besides, I found a used-up cigarette up there, and I know it was you who used it up."

She just freezes and looks at me in amazement. I know I have her, so I slam the door and walk away. As I clomp back downstairs, I think how much of a loser Penny is, and then I think, *Jeez, even my Mom forgets my birthday!*

I'm getting the strong feeling that everyone has forgotten that I'm thirteen today. But a small part of me thinks they're just trying to fool with me. I go outside and throw walnuts at the ammonia tank for a while, then go back into the house since it's nearly lunchtime, expecting maybe Pauly and June Bug to jump out at me, blowing kazoos and throwing streamers and balloons up in the air. But all I find is Pauly at the table. He's resting his bandaged foot up on the table and eating a stupid hot dog.

"Hey, P.P.," says Pauly. "They-ohs an extwa hot dog foh you in the mic-wo-wave."

"Gee, thanks, Pauly," I say. "Where's everybody else?"

"They took a hohse wide."

"Why didn't you go?"

"They said I'm too little."

I grab the dog out of the microwave, shove it into my mouth in two bites, without even putting it in a bun, and then I drink a big glass of water from the sink. "I'm going to run over to Jimmy's," I say to Pauly. "If anyone cares where I am."

"Can I come?" he says.

"No," I say.

"But I'm bohd."

"You're a bird?"

"No," he says, "bohhh-wed like, I can't think of anything to do."

"Tough nuggets," I say and walk out.

When I get to Jimmy's, I find him, surprise, surprise, shooting baskets in his machine shed. I walk up and say hey, but he doesn't answer back, just glances at me and nods. He's wearing dirty jeans and a white tank top undershirt that's got dirt all over it. Around his head is a red bandana. He looks pretty cool. I jump in and start rebounding for him. He's doing mostly bank shots today, and making nearly every one. His hoop is pretty cool. It's got this wooden backboard that's painted black, and on the part where's there's usually a square painted above the rim, there's a red and black bull's-eye instead. And the rim's net is chain, not regular rope or whatever. The whole thing is connected to the ceiling of the machine shed by this complicated-looking contraption that looks like it hoists everything up into the ceiling when you're done shooting. I start to sweat because I'm really hustling after the ball. Jimmy shoots and shoots, and the sound of the ball banking off that bull's-eye and going through the chain net makes a nifty sound. *Donk, kish. Donk, kish.* Finally, he takes a break.

We walk over to this old pump and Jimmy raises the handle up and down until water comes out. He fills his mouth and then ducks his head under the water. He shakes his hair like a dog, and it splatters me. "Go ahead," he says.

I take a drink and wet my head. It feels great. Jimmy dips his head under again and shakes his mane.

"It's my birthday today," I say.

Jimmy takes another drink, a long one this time. He belches. "How old?" he says.

"Thirteen," I say.

Jimmy raises his eyebrows. Then he turns and walks back to the machine shed and picks up his ball. I follow. He starts dribbling it, fancy stuff, behind his back, between his legs, quick little dribbles that remind me of the fast chickens at Uncle Stretch's.

"Hey, Jimmy," I say. "I got a favor to ask."

Jimmy stops dribbling and says, "Stretch already called my dad and asked. Yeah, I'll drive you to the state fair. We'll leave Friday at noon."

"Awesome!" I say. "I gotta go."

"See ya," Jimmy says, and takes a shot. *Donk, kish!*

On the way back home, I decide to jog. I need to keep in shape. I don't even care that everybody forgot my birthday since Jimmy's taking me up to the state fair. It's gonna be great. I ramp up my speed. When I look back, little puffs of dust are coming up from my feet because I'm running so fast.

When I get to the yard, I can smell someone grilling. Pork chops or steaks. It smells so good. Again, the idea that they might be having a surprise party for me pops into my head. I go in the house, and in the dining room, everyone's sitting at the table, eating. There's all kinds of food on the table—pork chops, beans, a big red JELL-O. But no birthday cake.

"Where you been?" asks Uncle Stretch.

"I was at Jimmy's, asking," I say. "I told Pauly to tell you."

Everyone looks at Pauly, who says, "Oops, I foh-got."

"Well, there's something else you all forgot, too," I say, my voice catching. All the sudden I feel like I might cry! "It's my birthday today!"

June Bug and Pauly stare at me. Uncle Stretch and Sheryl stare at me, then at each other. Then they stare at Penny. Penny stares at me. "No, it isn't!" she says.

"Today's August thirteenth!" I say. "We're thirteen!"

"You doughnut," says Penny. "Today's the eleventh."

"No, it's not!" I say. "Today's the thirteenth, our birthday!"

Uncle Stretch sighs, cuts a piece of meat, and puts it in his mouth. He chews a few times. "It's the eleventh, Son," he says.

"No, it's not!" I say. "I think I would know."

"There's a calendar magnet on the fridge," says June Bug, pointing.

I stomp over and look. The print is tiny, but it's clear. I feel like tearing the refrigerator door off the hinges. "You sure the year's right on this thing?"

"Would it make you feel better if we sang you 'Happy Birthday' ahead of schedule?" asks June Bug.

"Very funny, Loon Bug," I say. I walk out of there and think how refreshing it would be never to see their faces again.

Chapter 20

PENNY CELEBRATES HER BIRTHDAY

Dear Diary,

It's August thirteenth.

Today, I am officially a teenager. And *today was the best birthday of my life*! Yesterday, I got a text from Wesley saying that he was riding Mick over, so when I got up this morning, I got myself really pretty, even prettier than normal by parting my hair on the side and clipping it with a barrette June Bug and Sheryl got me for my birthday. They don't usually have good taste because they wear all their gaudy stuff at once, but if you wear just one or two shiny things at a time, then it looks nice and not trashy. I hope they both take a hint from me and tone it down.

The barrette has a brownish-amber stone in the middle, surrounded by yellowish-green stones all around. It's really pretty and looks good in my hair.

After I did my hair and put on a little blush and mascara, I went downstairs, where Pauly and June Bug and Sheryl and Uncle Stretch were waiting for Percy and me. They pulled out our chairs and served up orange juice, pancakes, and bacon. I passed on the bacon because I don't like to eat meat anymore, and I must be influencing Sheryl because she said, "Me neither!" She smiled at me, and she nodded to the refrigerator where she had hung the note I wrote her about smoking. Rather than get mad and defensive about it, she said that I was right and that she was going to put it in a place where she would have to read it several times a day.

Side note: At first it was hard for me to sit near Percy after he rudely interrupted me in my room the other day and accused me of smoking that cigarette. I have been thinking long and hard about that, and have decided to forgive him, but just not tell him that I forgive him. He deserves to be forgiven, and I do, too. (I just don't know how he found out, exactly, and I will have to watch him more closely.)

Then Sheryl actually had a really good idea when she told everyone to take a turn telling the rest of the family their favorite quality about me and Percy. Pauly said he really liked when Percy played football with him and threw the ball like a real football player, and then he said he really liked it when I read stories to him. It's true that I've read to Pauly a lot, but I didn't know that Pauly liked it, since half the time he'd be staring off into space, or interrupting with off-topic questions, or even falling asleep.

It goes to show that you never know when a kid might be paying attention. This summer, I already read *Fantastic Mr. Fox*, *Charlotte's Web*, *James and the Giant Peach*, *Because of Winn-Dixie*, and a handful of Goosebumps books to him. Usually, I have to force him to sit down and listen. I tell him that kids who are read to are about a thousand times smarter than kids who aren't read to and that I'm doing it for his own good. So, that was a nice surprise.

June Bug said she liked playing outside with Percy and that I gave good advice sometimes. This is true, because I recently gave her some really good advice on her hair and makeup and clothes. I've also given her plenty of good advice about how to stay healthy, and even Sheryl must agree, because she hasn't smoked a cigarette in ages. Then it was Sheryl's turn, and she said she was so grateful for Percy and me because we've brought so much vitality (she actually used that word, which totally amazes me) back to the farm and back to our Uncle Stretch. Then it was Uncle Stretch's turn, and it sounded like this:

Stretch: (Scratching his head and squinting for a long while like he couldn't think of anything to say.) Percy, you've shaped up quite a bit over that past couple months. Keep it up.

Percy: (Looking real proud.) Thanks, Uncle Stretch.

Stretch: (Looking at me and smiling an actual smile.) Penny, you remind me of your mother more and more every day . . . but you've still got a long way to go.

Me: (Thinking that his compliment sort of sounded like a backhanded insult, but accepting that it's about as good as it gets with Stretch.) Thanks, Uncle Stretch.

After breakfast, Percy and I got to open our present from Uncle Stretch, which was wrapped up in a tarp and sitting outside. Basically, we didn't have to unwrap it. All we had to do was lift it up to see that he got us a trampoline! We said it was awesome, and I gave him a hug. That was the first time I hugged him or any man besides my dad, and it wasn't too bad. Then Sheryl went back inside to make us some birthday cake and take a rest. Pauly and Uncle Stretch and June Bug and Percy got to work on the trampoline, which was in about a trillion pieces.

I climbed up the windmill a ways. I like to sit up

there and just look around at all the fields and groves and roads and the river. I was also hoping to get another text message, but it turned out I didn't need one, because before lunch, I could see Wesley riding toward our place on Mick and pulling another horse alongside him. I climbed down and ran out to the end of the driveway to meet them. Here was our conversation:

Wesley: (Looking *very* cute in a Zombie Cowboy kind of way, with his black jeans and black boots.) Hey.
 Me: (Feeling nervous/happy/excited.) Hey, what's up?
 Wesley: (Smiling in a really intelligent-looking way.) Happy birthday.
 Me: Thanks.
 Wesley: (Holding up a brown paper bag.) I packed a lunch and brought Bud. Can you come?
 Me: (Trying not to appear too eager.) I'll ask.

Then I ran as fast as possible to the house and asked Sheryl, who said yes and gave me a funny smile. Then Wesley and I went for a ride together, and we had the most amazing day ever. Though I'd spent a lot of time feeding Bernie and Brenda, I'd never actually ridden a horse before. I was scared to ride Bud, but he was a way nicer horse than Bernie and Brenda and never tried to bite me or buck me off. Wesley said I was a natural.

I can't say we talked too much. Wesley's pretty quiet, and I, for one, am not a big talker. But sometimes it's just nice to be quiet with someone else and be comfortable, which is exactly how I felt about being with Wesley. We rode to the Rabbit River, which isn't too far away, but far enough away so Pauly and Percy couldn't spy on me, and then Wesley made a little picnic for us. He brought Cheez-Its and Gatorade and a big bag of M&M'S and some beef jerky (which I politely declined), and then he gave me another CD he made for me with all these old country-western songs he said his dad listens to, and he's learned to like, too. I'd never heard any of them before, and some of them were a little dirty, especially ones by this guy named Conway Twitty (what a weird name!).

Wesley looked so cool wearing his T-shirt and jeans and cowboy boots. I'm for sure in love. We didn't kiss or anything because I'm not ready for that kind of a relationship, but we threw grass at each other, and he kicked me in the leg when I made a joke about how his hair looked like a Dairy Queen treat in the front.

Then we rode back, and June Bug and Percy and Pauly were waiting for us. Then we all five jumped on the new trampoline and practiced doing flips and stuff until dinnertime, when Stretch said it was time for Wesley to head home. I helped him get his horses ready and said it'd be fun to see him again sometime. He said that sounded good, which means he'll probably come back soon or at least probably text me tomorrow. I thought June Bug would be all jealous and maybe even try to steal Wesley from me, but she was really cool and said I was lucky and wanted to know if she could listen to the CD he made for me. I told her that we could all listen to it after supper.

Sheryl made cream of wild rice soup because that's Percy's favorite and avocado soft tacos because those are my favorite. Mom called right near the end of supper and told us she loved us and that her appeal looked to be going well. She told me she was really, really sorry about not being here for our birthday. She told me how proud she was of me. She told me she missed me and my brothers so much it made her teeth hurt, and she couldn't wait to wrap her arms around me. She told me to close my eyes and try and imagine the big, big hug she was sending through the phone. I did, and I swear I could really feel it.

It was nice to hear her voice and remember that hers was the first important voice Percy and I heard thirteen years ago. Then I remembered that this was our first birthday apart from her, which made me pretty sad.

After we hung up, Sheryl asked how our mother was

and how she sounded. Then she asked at what time Percy and me had been born. I told her I didn't know. But then Uncle Stretch said he knew. He said that he was there.

Percy: What? You mean you saw me buck naked?
Stretch: Don't you guys know your own birth story?

We shook our heads, and I started to get real excited because since Uncle Stretch hardly ever even talks, I knew this story must be very important and interesting.

Here's what happened the night we were born, according to Uncle Stretch, who was *there*! (All the following words came out of Uncle Stretch's mouth, so I will try to write it like he said it. But he sometimes mumbles, uses weird phrases no one has heard of, or uses crassness, so forgive me if this isn't exactly right or appropriate!)

Stretch: (Scratching at his face, which looks like it hasn't been shaved in about a week.) You two don't 'member your grandparents, but this is their place we're livin' on. Before that it was my pops's pops's place and so on. He was born in this house. His pops was born in this house. All the way back. Even those old horses were born on this place.

Stretch: (Reclining in his chair and making his hands like a hammock behind his head.) Yer mama, Danielle, married Allen despite what we all wanted. None of us really liked him much. Now I know you kids get all jumpy when I start talkin' 'bout yer dad, but the guy just rubs me the wrong way and always has. That don't have nothin' to do with you three. So quit takin' it personal. My ma, yer grandma, got real upset and quit talkin' to Danielle entirely when it happened. They didn't speak for upwards of 'bout three years. They're both stubborn women, I guess.

Stretch: My pops did what my ma did because she was a yeller, and so we didn't hear a word from Danielle until she showed up one day in the summer, her belly out to here. (Moving his hands from behind head and simulating a fake belly.) Ready to explode with you two. I was livin' here with Roland, who musta been 'bout twelve or thirteen, I guess. Same age as you kids now.

Stretch: I'd been havin' troubles with Kim. Kim was my wife for a good many years, though I can't say many of the years were good. She'd took off to California to think things over and never came back. I worked at the lumberyard in town in those days, so Roland and me had moved back in here with Ma and Pops, so they could keep an eye on Roland while I worked.

Stretch: (Crossing his legs to the side of the table and looking off into a far corner of the room.) Anyway, Ma was not going to let Danielle stay and said some nasty things. Ma could be a hard and unreasonable woman. But Danielle told her to get over it and quit freezin' her out. Danielle told Ma that only uneducated hicks act nasty to their own family. Danielle said that learnin' that people can disagree and still get along is somethin' it was high time that Ma learned because she was about to be a grandma again, and your ma didn't want an old crab bein' the grandma to her kids.

Stretch: (Breathing deeply, as though he still can't quite believe that our mother had spoken to her mother in that way.) That's what she said, and Pops and I about fell out of our chairs, 'cause nobody ever talked to Ma like that. Ma looked ready to kill someone but then started laughin' and moved Danielle back into her old room. (Smiling a smile that makes his face look like a little boy's, somehow.) Just like that, the feud was over.

Stretch: (Turning his face more serious again.) It wasn't a week later that Danielle woke us all up in the middle of the night, sayin' she needed to get to the doctor. Where Allen was during all this, I'm not too sure. That ministry of his was just gettin' goin', I think, and had him travelin' all over roundin' up parishioners and money and whatnot. Anyway, it was pretty exciting business with Ma timin' Danielle's contractions, and Pops packin' up the truck to take yer ma to the hospital.

Stretch: (Grabbing a toothpick from the toothpick holder and jabbing at a tooth in the back of his mouth for a few seconds.) That old truck's engine was on its last leg, soundin' like a couple tail-tied bobcats fightin' under the hood. Between drivin' it from the shed to the house, it overheated, and Pops was a real stickler about not blowin' up engines, and so he said that that truck wasn't goin' anywhere. My car was in town at the shop, waitin' for a new compressor, and the only other vehicle suitable for road travel was the grain truck. So Pops started movin' the suitcases from the pickup truck to the grain truck, and in the meantime, Danielle went from zero to ten in pain and yellin'. She told us she was going to the bathtub and to call the ambulance because she wasn't gettin' in any vehicle with us yahoos.

Stretch: Found out later that she'd learned all about deliverin' babies in the years she was gone. She'd took up nursin' and was travelin' to all kinds of poor places with Allen. She'd learned this trick about water births and told Ma to fill up that tub with hot water because she was gettin' in. After that, I don't know much about what happened. The two women closed the bathroom door, and all we heard was Danielle shoutin' at Ma about what to do when you came out and some other wild noises. After a while, Ma opened up the door and passed Penny to me, wrapped in a towel. About five minutes later, she came out with Percy wrapped in a towel. Both of you babies was all red and lumpy-headed and had gunk all over you, but you were healthy, and we were happy for it.

Stretch: (Taking a drink of coffee.) The ambulance had to come all the way from the other side of the county and took near an hour. Before it got here, your mom had showered off and come out in a green sweat suit. She said she was glad that was over and asked what we thought of *Penelope* and *Perseus* for names. Ma said she'd prefer regular old *Michael* or *Jacob* for the boy. She also said that *Perseus* was the ugliest name she'd ever heard. Danielle told her that was just another uneducated judgment and to be quiet if she didn't know a good name that came from the cradle of civilization when she heard it.

Stretch: Ma went to bleach the tub, and the ambulance came to pick you three up. Then Ma came out and said the name wasn't too bad after all. Well, Perseus and Penelope you became. You all got checked out at the hospital and sent back here. You were here for a good couple of weeks before Allen showed up and packed you all up. Nearly broke Roland's little heart seein' you babies leave. He was a good one for keepin' you quiet by letting you suck on his pinky. After that, Danielle made phone calls home sometimes but mostly sent letters and postcards from wherever Allen was settin' up a church.

Stretch: (Scratching the side of his head.) Let's see now, you two were born the year before we had that big rain and flood. Roland had his accident five years after the flood. Ma died the spring after Roland, and Pops 'bout six months later. I nearly lost my mind with grief and loneliness the next handful of years till Sheryl and June Bug here saved me from drinkin' myself to death. And now that you all showed up and saved me from dyin' of a broken heart, I feel like things have been practically just right.

With that, Stretch's eyes got all glassy, and he picked himself up and said he needed to go to the bathroom. We all just sat there quiet (even Percy) until he came out again, and then he started to eat his dessert like nothing had happened, so we ate ours, too, and eventually, Percy and Pauly and June Bug started jabbering like usual.

I didn't want to move a muscle the whole time Stretch was talking for fear he'd stop. I've gotten pretty used to sitting still and pretending to be listening intently to preaching and praying and such, but I was really, sincerely listening to Stretch.

Here are the most interesting parts of that story: For one, Percy and I were born right here in this house, in the downstairs bathroom! I'll never look at that tub the same again. For two, sometimes I forget that Percy and I are twins and that we're connected to each other in a way most people can't possibly understand. He really drives me crazy, but I have to admit that he seems to be maturing just a tiny, little bit. For three, Grandma sounds a lot like me in that she liked to keep things spic-and-span clean. For four, this isn't the first time Daddy abandoned us. He abandoned us before we were even born! For five, my life was in Stretch's hands almost immediately after I came out, and I survived! For six, Stretch has been through some really, really hard times, and I'm going to do my best to be a good niece to him now so he never feels like his family is going to abandon him again. I know what it's like to be abandoned, and it is not a good feeling.

Chapter 21
Percy at the State Fair

JIMMY'S twenty minutes late to pick me up for our drive to the state fair so I can show Hercules II. I'm looking out the window, waiting like crazy while Uncle Stretch keeps giving me all these annoying extra instructions. *Make sure to feed and water your chicken extra if it's hot. Be polite to all the people you meet. Don't be messing around at the fair. Keep your nose clean. No swearing. No fighting. Did you pack your chicken-grooming tools? You bring along a belt for those jeans? Now, where's that money I gave you—you put it in your wallet? You got a wallet, right?* He paces back and forth, then he stops and acts like he just remembered something real important. "No smoking or drinking," he says.

"Gimme a break," I say. "I'm only thirteen."

"There's kids younger'n you that could've used that advice," he says.

I wonder who he's thinking about, but I don't want to encourage him.

Uncle Stretch has already given me two hundred and fifty bucks to pay for hotel, food, gas, and any emergencies. He said he expects a return of at least a hundred bucks if no emergencies arise. He called around to find a cheap hotel for us to stay at, and he wrote out some directions to get there. His handwriting is very small and messy. It's written in cursive that doesn't even look like real letters—it's more like tiny tumbleweeds with smoke coming off them—but if I complain I can't read it, he might bother me with some more dumb stuff.

Finally, at 7:55 a.m., Jimmy drives up in his car. I load Hercules II, who's in a cage, and put my other stuff in, too, including the new football I got for my birthday. Uncle Stretch goes over to Jimmy, puts his hand on his shoulder, and tells him some stuff in a voice too low for me to hear. Within a few minutes, we're out of the driveway and off to the Twin Cities. It'll be about a two-hour trip.

Jimmy's car is a little white beater that smells like dust. There are lots of empty Gatorade bottles on the floor and other trash. I'd been imagining he'd have a sweet black car with leather seats or something. But it's okay. I've been awaiting this day for quite a while, hoping Jimmy and I will have some great conversations on the way up, but Jimmy doesn't look much like talking.

I decide that if there's going to be any great conversation, I may have to ask the first question. "Stretch called you a punk the other day at the dinner table," I say. "Does that make you mad?"

"Most sixteen-year-olds are punks," says Jimmy.

"Even you?"

"Probably."

"He says you smoke and drink."

"I don't drink anymore. It's what killed my brother. And it gets in the way of basketball."

"What are you playing for? Stretch says you're not even on the high school team."

"The coach is an idiot. I'm aiming for college ball."

"How are people going to see you? Like, college coaches?"

"YouTube."

"Huh."

It's quiet awhile except for the rattle of Jimmy's car.

"What else do you do for fun?" I ask.

"I have this girlfriend I hang out with some. And I listen to music and paint and read books."

"I draw a lot," I say. "Check this out." I reach over

the seat into my duffel bag and pull out my sketch-book and flip it to the page where I drew Elle with her arm down and her breast showing.

"Wow," says Jimmy. "Nice nudie."

I turn red and smile.

"No," says Jimmy. "That's a really good picture, Pers. Can tell you've got some talent."

We drive for about a minute without speaking. My whole body feels warm, and it's not just the sun coming through the window that's making me feel that way.

"What's your girlfriend's name?" I ask.

"Riley."

"Is she hot?"

"What would you know about hot?"

"I don't know," I say, getting embarrassed. "Elle—I mean, the lady in the picture I drew—she's hot."

Jimmy grins. "Riley's all right. Fairly hot. When she's older, she'll be really hot."

"What do you paint?" I ask.

"Dark stuff."

"What kind of books do you read?"

"Mostly short stories. Poe, O. Henry, Hemingway. The masters. Poe's the best."

"Who's Poe?"

"Poe's the best," repeats Jimmy. "Edgar Allan Poe. Wrote this story called 'The Black Cat' that'll make you shudder, you're so scared, if you think deep about it. Messes with your mind."

"What happens?"

"This animal lover guy who just got married gets a black cat but then starts to hate it because the cat follows him everywhere and annoys him, so he kills it. But the cat comes back—like a ghost—so he tries killing it again but ends up killing his wife—chops her in the head with an axe."

"Whoa."

"He buries her inside his basement wall so nobody will find out, but when the police come to investigate, they hear something crying from behind the wall, rip it open, and there's the cat, still alive, and the dead, head-axed body of the guy's dead wife."

"Whoa."

"Yeah, whoa. But the part that messes with you is why did the guy change from fun-loving animal guy to dark-minded axe murderer? Like, how do people go from good to bad so easily? It can't just be because of some stupid cat. Something in his soul wanted to be a killer, wanted to be bad. It happens all the time if you watch people."

"Did you turn into a punk when your brother died?"

"No."

"I thought I might turn evil when my mom and dad abandoned me."

Jimmy doesn't say anything.

"Uncle Stretch says you're a punk but you've got a good heart," I say. "But maybe your heart will turn bad."

"No."

"How do you know?"

"Because I care about everyone and couldn't stand it if I was a jerk."

"How do you know it'll always be that way?"

"Just do," says Jimmy. "Hey, dig up that CD case under the seat."

I do. He takes it from my hand and flips through it with one hand while steering the car with the other. He puts a CD into the player and cranks the volume. The guitars and drums are sort of slow, and the guy singing has a sad, gravelly voice. I've heard people with better voices than his.

"What's this music?" I yell over to Jimmy.

"This is the blues, boy," shouts Jimmy.

He puts on a cool-looking pair of sunglasses and reaches past me to pop open the glove box. He grabs an old-fashioned pair of sunglasses and drops them in my lap, and then he digs out a plastic bag of sunflower seeds. He loads up a bunch into his cheek and says I can have some if I want. He spits the shells into an empty bottle he finds at his feet. I take a few seeds and grab an empty Gatorade bottle for myself. It's a sunny day out, and we're whizzing by lots of cars. Huge clouds look like giant football players, some smashing into each other, some running away. The music feels like it's inside of my brain and vibrating in my heart. The gravel-voiced guy is saying some pretty cool lines, and I decide I like his style. I check the backseat and see Hercules II bobbing his head in his cage, and it looks like he's grooving to the music.

After about an hour, Jimmy turns down the music and says, "You bring your swimsuit?"

"Yeah," I say, "but I don't think there's a pool at the hotel Stretch picked out for us."

Jimmy makes a couple of turns, and I see a sign that says, WISCONSIN AND THE APPLE RIVER WELCOME YOU.

"Wisconsin?" I say.

"Ever been tubing?" says Jimmy.

"No."

"You're about to."

"I think we're supposed to check into the hotel at, um . . . ," I say, checking my notes from Stretch.

"Don't worry about that," says Jimmy. He parks the car and says, "Here's where you hurry up and change into your swimsuit."

"In the car?"

"Yeah," he says, "hurry up. No one's looking."

"Are you going to change?"

"Already wearing mine," he says.

"What about that van over there?" I say. "I think I can see some people looking over here."

"No one wants to see your little pocket trout," Jimmy says. "Now hurry up."

I try to hurry, but I keep getting my toes caught in that netting underwear in my suit. I look at Jimmy a couple of times to make sure he's not spying on me. He isn't. Finally, my suit's on, and I tie up the string.

Jimmy goes around to the trunk. "Take your bag and stuff and bring it over here," he says. I do, and he throws it in the trunk along with his stuff. He rolls down a window and says, "This bird'll be okay if we give him a little air, won't he?"

"I suppose," I say. "Is there a bathroom around here?"

Jimmy points. "Use that big tree over there."

I run over and water the big tree. I look around to make sure nobody saw anything.

We walk a ways to this shack, and Jimmy pays a fat lady some money for two big, black, rubber inner tubes. I follow Jimmy down to the river's edge, and he flops his tube out in the water, jumps on it, and begins to slowly float away.

"Come on, kid!" he says.

I get nervous trying to jump in the water and sort

of fall in. My sunglasses slip off, and while I look for them, my tube gets away from me and begins drifting away, toward Jimmy.

"Swim after it!" says Jimmy.

I forget the glasses and take a little dive into the water. It's cold! I come up for air and start swimming. The river pushes me along, and it seems like I'm swimming really fast. I catch up to my tube and hold on to the edge.

"You gotta sit in the middle," says Jimmy.

He's floating so far on up ahead that I can barely hear him. I wrestle my tube a little and finally get seated. I paddle my hands on the sides to try and catch up. Finally, I do, only because Jimmy grabs on to a tree branch sticking out over the water. When I get even, Jimmy paddles himself right up next to me and hooks his arm in my tube.

"Now what happens?" I say.

"We float," he says.

It seems kind of boring at first, but soon I get used to it. We pass big groups of people who float slower because they're all linked up, and we pass people who've stopped to swim. Some of the swimmers are girls, or women. When Jimmy and I go by, I can see Jimmy pretending not to look, but I know he really is. You can pretend good when you're wearing sunglasses like Jimmy's. Some people say hi to us, and we wave back. A lot of the older people we see are drinking beer. One guy floats by us wearing a helmet with two cans of beer attached to the sides and straws bending down into his mouth. He's got his tube roped to another tube that holds a mangy red dog and a little cooler with beer. He digs out a can and throws it to Jimmy. "Cheers, young gun," he says.

"Thanks," says Jimmy. He hides the can of beer under the water as we cruise along.

"You're not gonna drink that, are you?" I say.

"Maybe," he says.

"You're not old enough," I say. "Isn't it illegal?"

Jimmy doesn't say anything.

I look at his hand holding the beer trailing under the surface of the water. The sun gleams off the silver can, and I can read the words OLD MILWAUKEE.

"Wish I had those glasses," I say, after a while.

"Wanna stop and swim?"

We stop at a low place in the river and put our tubes up on the bank. I see Jimmy looking at the beer and looking at me. I know he wants to drink it. Some girls float by in pink bikinis. "Hey, sexy!" one of them says to Jimmy. "Wanna come party?"

Jimmy just waves. Some older guys float by and wave, and Jimmy throws them the can of Old Milwaukee. "Thanks, buddy!" one of them yells.

We get back to floating again, and it's really nice,

but hot. Then some big clouds make it shadier, and it feels perfect. I'm trailing my hand in the water, feeling the river bottom when it gets low, sometimes picking up rocks. All of a sudden, I feel something. I jerk my hand out of the water, thinking it's a fish, but it's a pair of sunglasses.

"Hey, Jimmy!" I say. "Look!"

I hand him the glasses and he inspects them. "Ray-Bans," he says. "Nice."

"Maybe there's a lost and found somewhere," I say.

Jimmy looks at me. "Didn't you lose your glasses in the river?" he says.

"Yeah," I say.

"Well, now the river gave 'em back again."

It takes me a second to get what he's saying. I put the Ray-Bans on and relax in the river. What a beautiful day.

After a while, Jimmy says, "All right, out here," and he stands up. He catches me by surprise, and I have to scramble to get out. There's a big pile of tubes sitting at the river's edge, and Jimmy tosses his on top, so I do, too. I follow him to a little road where there's a bus waiting. We get on, and it takes us back to Jimmy's car.

When we get to the car, Jimmy takes out the keys and pops the trunk. He reaches in his bag and fishes out a pair of shorts and a shirt. Before I know what's going on, he whips off his trunks, and I'm left staring at his privates.

"Jeez!" I say, looking quickly away. "I saw everything, Jimmy."

"Grow up," he says.

I take out the outfit I was wearing earlier in the day and hurry to put it on.

"Uh-oh," Jimmy says.

I struggle with my zipper. "What?" I say.

"Your bird's vacated the premises."

"Huh?" I run over to where Jimmy's standing, staring at the backseat. The window's open wider than I remember, and Hercules II is definitely *not* in his cage. We search the car. No bird.

I look up into the surrounding trees before realizing that I've never seen a chicken in a tree.

"He's gone," Jimmy says. "Long gone."

Chapter 22
PENNY AND THE WHIRLWIND

Dear Diary,

I know staring is rude, but I can't stop looking at Uncle Stretch and thinking about that year when basically his whole family died. I must have been bugging him because he told me that if I didn't knock it off, he was going to knock me alongside the head, which he might do but not in a mean way. One thing I've learned about Uncle Stretch is that his bark is worse than his bite.

I keep thinking about Kim and wondering what got into her that would make her leave her husband and child. I know prying is rude, but I asked Sheryl about it, and she said that Kim was real pretty and always wanted to be an actress or bikini model. Sheryl said that Stretch only heard from her a handful of times after she left in the first year and then not at all after that. Kim didn't tell anyone, not even her parents, where she was.

After Roland's death, some of her relatives went out to California to track her down. When they found her, she was waitressing at a seafood café and living with a guy she called her agent. She took Roland's death real hard and said to tell Stretch she just couldn't do it. "Couldn't do what?" I asked Sheryl. But Sheryl said she didn't know. So then I asked her how Stretch could stand it, the not knowing. Then Sheryl called me honey and said that sometimes people can't or won't give you the answers that you want. Sheryl said that sometimes the only thing you can do is keep going forward and living your life the best that you can.

You wouldn't ever know it by looking at her, but sometimes Sheryl's good to talk to and pretty smart.

Then something even more interesting happened. Since Percy had gone to the fair with Jimmy, I thought I'd do a good deed and clean out his room in the granary, not because I wanted to snoop but because he never cleans it, and it's probably just boiling over with germs and diseases. It's nothing short of a miracle that Percy hasn't come down with mad cow disease or mastitis. I made a nice hot bucket of soapy water and told Pauly to come and help me because Sheryl looked like she was at her wit's end. Pauly's always in her hair when she's trying to get some cooking or cleaning done.

We went into the granary, and I was right. Percy's room was a total disaster area. So first, Pauly and I picked up his clothes off the floor and put them in a hamper to be washed (Sheryl does all the clothes washing, but June Bug and I hang them on the line and fold them up). Then we opened up the closet and found *more* clothes all over the floor. Way in the back of the closet, I saw a little box against the wall. I thought it probably held Percy's drawings of football guys or soldiers, but on the top it said, ROLAND.

Well, obviously, I couldn't help but look inside. I mean, who could blame me, right? But when I opened the box, it was empty except for an old, creased photograph. It was of Stretch and a woman I assume to be Kim, and Roland, who looked around seven or eight, maybe. He was wearing a big Native American headdress, and on the back of the picture, it said *Rolly, Indian Chief*. Stretch was wearing jeans and a western shirt, and Kim was wearing a cute purple dress and a necklace with a shiny silver cross pendant. All three of them were smiling really big, like someone just told them a hilarious joke.

At first, I found myself wondering how a guy like Stretch could get a woman with such a nice body and cheekbone structure. But after staring at the photo for a while, I came to decide she wasn't all that. I mean, she had a nice face, but her hair looked overprocessed and way too blond and dry and split-ended, especially for her tan, tan skin. And though her figure looked pretty good, I wondered if it was really a curse, since her idea that she was pretty enough to be a model was what made her leave. The cross pendant bothered me. It seemed sacrilegious. Who did she think she was?

I can't understand why Kim would leave her family. At the time this photo was taken, was she already thinking about being a bikini model or actress instead of a wife to Stretch and a mom to Roland? Was she already making plans to hightail it to California? Was she faking that big smile that showed her teeth, or *was* she actually happy? Maybe her unhappiness hadn't yet dawned upon her. Maybe at the time of this photo, she hadn't yet realized that she didn't want to live in the middle of nowhere anymore and be a wife and mother. Maybe she hadn't yet considered that her life might be better as a bikini model.

So then I wondered about Roland. I wondered how often he sat right in this same spot and thought about his mother the way I've sat and thought about mine. I wondered if he thought about being abandoned all the time the way I do. Even though Mom didn't try to get arrested, she *did* get arrested, and that *did* make her abandon us and she *should* have known better. Even though Dad probably didn't abandon us on purpose at first, he *did* abandon us because he eventually chose to go to Hawaii with Peggy, the accountant. I thought about how very similar my situation and Roland's situation were. And all of this made me think that Roland and I could have been really good friends.

It's just hard to figure out the motives of adults. Do they know they are going to do bad things on purpose or do the ideas just come all of a sudden and they can't help themselves? I'll bet Roland spent hours looking at the picture I found in the shoe box and wondering whether his mom was faking being happy or whether she really *was* happy.

I guess you just have to be happy when the moment is happy and not expect it to be a lifetime contract. I, for one, am going to take happiness day by day from now on.

Dear Mom,

I don't want you to get jealous or anything, but I've been getting along pretty well with Sheryl. She's actually a nice person, even though she doesn't dress all that great and sets a bad example that way for June Bug. I don't think of her as my mother, but I guess I don't mind thinking of her as a favorite aunt-type person. Sometimes it's easier to talk to adults who are almost like parents but aren't.

I've been thinking a lot about Stretch and his family. His wife might have had postpartum depression, and maybe that's why she ran away from Stretch and Roland. One symptom of that is disinterest in the child, which you would definitely have to be able to leave your child like that. I guess she didn't know it, but there are medications for it. Too bad you weren't around at the time, since you're pretty good at finding medicines for people! Or she could have had bipolar disorder, which gives people grandiose ideas about themselves. Believing that you could run off to California to be an actress or bikini model after you've already been married and had a kid is a grandiose idea. Too bad Stretch didn't know the symptoms, or he could have just told Kim it was postpartum or bipolar and saved himself a lot of heartache. But then I guess he wouldn't have met Sheryl, who seems to make Stretch happy, or at least as happy as Stretch can be since he hardly ever talks or smiles.

I suppose you heard that Percy and Pauly almost got struck by lightning. Their close encounter with death has really got me thinking. So, I've decided to break up with Wesley. He's been a nice boyfriend and everything, but how do I know he's the best one? How do I know there isn't another better boyfriend out there? For instance, there's this older boy named Jimmy. How do I know he's not better than Wesley? I don't want to accidentally get married to the wrong person right away.

For example, in *Zombie Cowboy, Book Three,* Patience Lonelyheart is saved from marrying the evil, rich vampire Handle Boomton because Eamon Cloversniffer drives a horseshoe through his heart, which is about the only way you can kill a vampire for good. But Patience Lonelyheart has met this other guy, a normal man who isn't a vampire, werewolf, or zombie, but who is a regular rancher and who can give her a normal life. So Eamon Cloversniffer makes the ultimate sacrifice and tells her that he is leaving town without her. He tells Patience to forget all about him as their love is impossible because he, Eamon Cloversniffer, is doomed to walk the earth forever as a zombie cowboy, and she is a regular mortal, who will grow old and eventually die. He tells her that she can live peacefully with the rancher and that she should marry him, have kids, and be happy.

That story just goes to show you that you can think you're in love and maybe be in love for a while, but another person might someday cross your path who might be a better fit. So, I'm going to explore all my options while I'm young. I think both you and Stretch would've been better off if you had shopped around a little more instead of just settling for the first person who showed the slightest bit of interest in you.

Love,
Penny

DEAR OKONKWO,

THANK YOU FOR YOUR RECENT LETTER. I WISH I COULD SEND SOME EXTRA MONEY TO HELP YOUR FATHER GET HIS INTERNET BUSINESS OFF THE GROUND. BUT I DON'T HAVE ANY EXTRA MONEY, AND IF I DID, I WOULD PROBABLY GET MYSELF INTERNET SO I WOULDN'T ALWAYS HAVE TO GO TO THE LIBRARY IN TOWN AND LISTEN TO SISTER ALICE SHUFFLE AROUND IN HER BLACK NUN HABIT!

WHAT'S THE NAME OF YOUR RELIGION, ANYWAY? I'M NOT ASKING BECAUSE I WANT TO TALK YOU OUT OF IT. I'M JUST CURIOUS. I'VE BEEN THINKING ABOUT RELIGION CONSTANTLY LATELY. I USED TO THINK ABOUT MY DADDY AND HIS CHURCH A LOT AND ASSUME THAT I WAS TAKING STOCK OF MY SPIRITUAL RELATIONSHIP WITH GOD. IT TURNS OUT THAT I WAS MOSTLY JUST THINKING ABOUT DADDY AND HIS CHURCH. AT THE TIME, IT SEEMED LIKE THE RIGHT WAY TO GO. I'M STARTING TO

THINK IT WASN'T, WHICH IS VERY CONFUSING
TO ME.

I'VE TRIED REALLY HARD TO BE AN OBEDIENT
DAUGHTER AND A GOOD CHRISTIAN. IT'S BEEN
REALLY HARD FOR ME TO REALIZE THAT NOT
EVERYTHING MY DADDY DOES IS RIGHT. I'VE
ALSO REALIZED THAT SOME OF THE STUFF THAT
GOD, THE FATHER, RECOMMENDS IN THE BIBLE
IS NOT RIGHT, LIKE SMITING CHILDREN. DO YOU
EVER FEEL THAT WAY? DO YOU EVER THINK THAT
YOUR FATHER MIGHT BE WRONG? HOW DOES IT
MAKE YOU FEEL?

SINCERELY,

PENELOPE PRIBYL

Chapter 23
Percy and the Tornado

YESTERDAY was one of the best days of my
life. Well, except for the part about losing track of
Hercules II. After tubing at the Apple River, we went
to a used bookstore in Minneapolis, where Jimmy
bought me an old comic book and a book of Poe.
Then we shot some baskets on a city court where all
these tough guys who were playing let Jimmy into a
game, and he did awesome. After that, we went to
Jimmy's uncle's house, where we played catch with my
new football until dark, when Jimmy's uncle started a
fire, roasted us some hot dogs, and pulled out his
guitar. Jimmy brought his guitar out, too, and after a
while, they were playing together, and it seemed like
they were just making things up, different strums and

words and stuff. They said it was the blues. They even let me sing a song. I said I didn't know what to sing about, so Jimmy's uncle just said, "Sing about your problems." So I did.

I sang about my lost chicken and my dead chicken, and I sang about how Pauly ticks me off, and how Penny is boring, and how Uncle Stretch thinks I'm lazy, but he doesn't even know me. I sang about how I miss my mom and my dad. I sang about rainy days and falling down and when you can't think of anything to do because you're bored. Once I got going, the song lasted about twenty minutes.

When the song was over, Jimmy's uncle laughed and called my song "The Percy Blues." We decided to stay at Jimmy's uncle's instead of a hotel. I had a great time. Even though I knew yesterday would be great, I was thinking it would be great in a certain way, but it was good in a very different way than I expected, and that's one of the things that made it so good. I stayed up until 3 a.m., which would have been a personal record if I hadn't stayed up all night long one time in Africa when we thought some bad guys were going to light the village on fire.

Today, when I got up, I wondered what the heck we had even been going to the fair for. Jimmy's uncle made us some omelets. I asked where his wife was, and he said, "She left in eighty-two." Then he made us some bacon.

After we pack up and get in the car, I say to Jimmy, "Do you think they'll give me a ribbon at the state fair because I lost my chicken?"

"Why would they?" he says.

"Well, you know. I got champion when Hercules the First died."

"You shouldn't've."

"But the judge killed it!"

"Sounds like your bird was pretty wild, dude."

"Who told you that?"

"Stretch."

"Figures. He's always talking bad things about me behind my back."

Jimmy turns and looks me in the eye. "Stretch doesn't care about making you look bad. He tells the truth. Your chicken *was* wild. That's the truth."

"Uncle Stretch hates me."

"He doesn't hate you. He's probably annoyed by you, though."

"Why?"

"You're annoying."

"Gee, thanks a lot, Jimmy."

"It's hard not to be annoying when you're a kid."

"Were you annoying?"

"Yep," says Jimmy. He turns up his CD player and loud guitars crash. "Still am!" he shouts.

We drive for a while before we get to the fair. We

park and have to walk a long ways before we get in. There are lots of sights and smells, but Jimmy walks us to the chicken barn. He asks some important-looking people where the judges are. We go over and find the people in charge and a bunch of kids checking in their chickens. These kids all have their hair combed, and their chickens are very calm and good-looking and big! Some of them look two times the size of Hercules I and II put together. If they got in a chicken fight with Hercules I or II, they'd whip some chicken butt.

"This here is Percy Pribyl," says Jimmy to a big guy with a green vest that says JUDGE. "He's scratching out of the chicken-showing competition."

The man in the green vest frowns at me. "Whatever for?" says the man.

"I let his bird loose yesterday at the Apple River while he was taking a pee," says Jimmy.

"You what?" I say.

The man just gives us bad looks.

Jimmy grabs me by the arm and says, "See ya," to the judge guy. We walk quickly away.

"You let out Hercules the Second on purpose?" I say.

"Yeah," says Jimmy. "I didn't feel like wasting time with him. Plus, you didn't deserve to be at this thing."

I'm so confused I don't really know what to say. Another reason I don't answer him is because Jimmy is ten times smarter than me, and most of the things I say to him sound, well, childish. We walk up to a little food stand and get in line.

"So what do we do now?" I say.

Jimmy hands me some meat on a poker thing. "We eat ribs on a stick," he says and takes a big bite from another poker thing. He looks like a wolf. A very cool wolf.

I take a bite, too. Sauce gets all over my cheek, but the meat tastes delicious. It's like food candy.

"Hey, Jimmy," I say. "I'm not mad at you for letting out Hercules the Second. The whole chicken thing with me getting invited to the state fair just because the judge killed my first chicken was just a big Horse Camp."

"So by *Horse Camp* you mean, like, a trick?"

"Sorta. Me getting grand champion was messed up. I'm not really that great at chicken showing."

"No kidding," says Jimmy. "And nice work with the horse camp metaphor. I like that."

We finish the ribs, and Jimmy buys us some Gatorades. Then we walk around for a while seeing lots of interesting things—people in weird costumes, a carrot as long as my arm, a sculpture of a princess made out of butter. The smells of delicious fried food fill my nose, and there's different kinds of music all over the place. It's great to be walking with Jimmy because I can almost feel the coolness rubbing off him onto me. But, all of a sudden, the sky gets dark, and the air goes from warm and still to cold and breezy.

Jimmy looks up at the sky. "Uh-oh," he says.

It starts to rain.

We run for cover under this tent thing that bunches of other people are huddled under, too. The rain starts coming heavy, and people are running everywhere, getting soaked to the skin. It's kind of fun watching them until a loud crack of thunder booms and lightning splits the sky.

"What do we do?" I yell to Jimmy.

"Gonna have to run for the car!" he says. "C'mon."

He starts sprinting, and I follow. There are already huge puddles in the way, and at first I try to dodge them like Adrian Peterson dodges tacklers when he's scoring touchdowns for the Minnesota Vikings, but then I just splash right through them because it's faster and there are too many. Jimmy jumps over some of the puddles, big, long leaps like a deer might make, and I notice his shoes aren't muddy at all, especially compared to mine.

Finally, we get to the car.

Inside, we're drenched. Jimmy fires up the engine and his CD player comes on, full blast. For a moment, it drowns out the rain pelting the car roof over our heads, but then Jimmy turns it way down.

"You had enough of the fair?" he says.

I shrug. "Sure."

Jimmy turns on his wiper blades, but even though they're going superfast, the rain makes the windshield blurry. Other people are clogging the parking lot, so Jimmy drives slow.

Finally, we get out onto the open road, and the rain lets up a little. The sky still looks really dark, almost green.

"What time is it?" I say.

"Why?" says Jimmy.

"I've never seen it so dark during the day."

Jimmy presses a button on his stereo and the numbers 12:05 show up. "Weather like this at high noon is not good," he says.

"What do you mean?" I say. I get a bad feeling in my gut.

"Storm weather," says Jimmy.

We drive awhile until we have to slow down because of a big line of cars in the way. "Turn on the radio," says Jimmy.

"How?" I say.

He punches a few buttons on his stereo, and a man's raspy voice comes over the scratchy airwaves. He is talking about a tornado sighted somewhere, when a police officer in a big black raincoat walks up and taps on Jimmy's window.

"We're turning people around," the officer says. "Tornado a few miles ahead knocked some power lines across the road. You boys head for safety."

"All right," says Jimmy. "Thanks." He rolls up the window.

"Whoa!" I say.

We get to a place up ahead where people are turning, and we follow them for a while. Then Jimmy takes a turn, and we have the road to ourselves all of a sudden.

"Are we heading home?" I say.

"Yeah, with a little detour," says Jimmy.

It's mostly quit raining, and the sky isn't quite as dark as it was. It's more yellowish now. Jimmy turns off the radio and puts on some of his music.

After a few miles, the sky gets green, and then black, and the rain starts pelting us again. Jimmy turns the radio back on, and the wiper blades are going crazy.

Jimmy's face looks a little scared.

"Are we gonna be all right?" I say.

Jimmy says nothing. He's concentrating, I suppose.

I'm looking out of my side window when I see a *huge* bolt of lightning. "Whoa!" I say. "Did you see that?"

Jimmy just keeps driving. The radio is fuzzy now, but Jimmy doesn't turn to something clearer.

Then he stops the car and says the worst swear word there is.

"What's wrong!" I say.

He points out his side window. A huge black cone is coming out of the sky.

"What is it?" I yell, but I already know.

"Twister," says Jimmy.

"Why aren't you driving?" I say.

"We need to get out now!" says Jimmy. He gets out and slams his door. I sit in my seat, frozen. I'm scared solid. The tornado sounds like a loud train. My door opens, and Jimmy yanks me out.

"C'mon!" he yells at me, and I notice his eyes seem really scared. "Run!" he yells, but I can barely hear him. I sprint after Jimmy, and it's like our feet aren't even hitting the earth. We're running down a road, toward a farmhouse. I look over and the tornado is about three football fields away. It's wider than it was at first, and the sound of it fills up my ears. It looks like it is *coming right after us!*

Jimmy turns around and yells something at me, but I can't hear it. The wind is about blowing us over. I look behind me at the tornado again and think I'm gonna die. I say a quick prayer to God in my head: *Please don't let me die, God! I'll be nice to Pauly for the rest of my life or whatever else you want. Please keep me safe!*

I follow Jimmy into a ditch and watch as he does a feetfirst baseball slide into a culvert beneath a little crossroad. He pokes his head out and waves me in. I sprint over, hit my knees, and reverse-crawl into the culvert. Jimmy pulls me back a few feet from the culvert's opening, next to him, and we lie there, almost side-by-side, packed tight in the small, circular space.

I look out the end of the culvert, and all I can see is black wind. The sound is horrible, like a train combined with an airplane combined with a thousand people moaning combined with ten thousand lions roaring. I look at Jimmy, and he's got his head down and his eyes closed. He's moving his lips. I put my head down and hope I don't die. I wonder if I am thinking the same thoughts as Roland did in the seconds before he stopped living.

In a couple of minutes, the roaring dies down. Jimmy crawls over me and out of the culvert, inch by inch. I follow. We stand up. The only sound is of rain falling quietly. I look back to where our car was. It's not there anymore. I look all around. I don't see it anywhere. The tornado's gone, too. All the corn in a field next to us is knocked straight down. A big piece of wall from a house or building is lying in the flattened corn. I follow Jimmy up to the road. I think we're too shocked to say anything. The farmhouse we were running toward doesn't look quite right. It's lopsided or something. We walk a ways farther. A cow lies in the ditch on its side, mooing. Its legs are all crooked.

"What do we do?" I say to Jimmy when we see it.

"Keep walking."

We walk and walk. In places, the land looks ripped. We walk some more.

Chapter 24
PeNNY COUNtS HeR BLeSSiNGS

Dear Diary,

Sometimes a person just has to open herself up to change and adapt to what the world has to offer. At the beginning of this summer, I couldn't have imagined my life without Dad, without the daily guidance of him and the church. I couldn't have imagined living on a farm with a bunch of people I'm barely related to. I can't believe how much has changed in such a short time. For a while there, I honestly thought I was going to develop a tumor or ulcer from all the stress, but it turns out I didn't. I've really matured physically, emotionally, and spiritually. I'm glad I kept this diary.

You might think I'd be nervous about starting

school in a new place, but I'm not. I've already got June Bug as a best friend and, by default, all her other friends have to like me, too, including Rachel, whom I haven't met yet, but I'm sure will like me since her first name is the same as my middle name.

The big commotion in the last week has revolved around the tornado that nearly killed Percy and Jimmy, this attractive boy who lives down the road. Excuse me if I don't go into great detail about it as everyone here is beyond bored with Percy mentioning the tornado at every opportunity. Here is an example of a conversation you might have with Percy:

You: (Smiling nicely.) Hello, Percy, how are you?

Percy: (Looking uneducated with missing front tooth.) I almost died last week from this deadly twister, so basically I'm just happy to be alive.

You: That's great. So what do you think of (fill in the blank)?

Percy: (Totally ignoring your question.) This deadly twister was, like, right on top of me, but I was holding on to Jimmy and hiding in a ditch so we wouldn't get sucked up like most normal, weak people would've if they were there.

You: Uh, cool.

Percy: Yeah, basically no one has probably ever

been inside a twister like that and survived, so I'm like one in ten million.

You: (Trying to send a message via body language that you wish he would change the subject.) That is great.

Percy: Uh-huh, you should have seen this thing! (Getting excited at his own words.) Blah, blah, blah . . . deadly twister . . . blah, blah, blah . . . deadly twister . . . blah, blah, blah . . . believe me, I was right in the middle of this thing . . . blah, blah, blah . . . deadly, horrifying, man-eating, annoying twister.

Honestly, he could go on for hours, and he has. I don't mean to insinuate that I'm not happy he survived or anything, but I, for one, wish he could be a little more humble about the whole episode. If I had escaped death, I would probably just be enjoying every minute of life thereafter, smelling flowers, listening to nature, looking deep into a horse's eye, and pondering all of the complexities of life, and wondering at this universe we've been placed in.

In other news, yesterday, June Bug and Sheryl took Percy, Pauly, and me on a tour of our new school. I'm very excited to be attending a regular school, and I know all the homeschool lessons Mom put me through will pay off. The school here is just a small place with one building housing all twelve grades. That's where I met Mr. Dalton, the English teacher who'll probably help me get my diary published. Mr. Dalton is gay, which you can kind of tell by the nice clothes he wears and his neat hair and fingernails, a stark contrast to most of the men around here who wear dirty jeans and don't shave unless they're going to a steak house for dinner. The old Penny would have looked at Mr. Dalton and worried about how and when to tell him his lifestyle is a big sin and that he would go to hell if he didn't change his ways. But the new Penny doesn't think or act with such judgment anymore. Sometimes, when I think about how judgmental and righteously indignant I was when I first got to Stretch's farm, I feel ashamed. Sometimes, I even feel like I should apologize to some people.

Mr. Dalton gave me a book to read called *The Good Earth,* by Pearl S. Buck. He said I'd like it, especially since the author was a lot like me. Her parents were missionaries, too. And her mother was a nurse who ministered to women and children. Apparently, Mr. Dalton must know all about our situation, compliments of Sheryl, no doubt, who can't help but blurt out every little thing that crosses hermind. But, Sheryl's big mouth does work in my favor sometimes, too. For instance, because Sheryl's a blabbermouth, I happen to know that Mr. Dalton has a partner who is a man and that they adopted a pair of twins who were born addicted to crack and who were the colicky-est babies ever and almost drove Mr. Dalton and his partner crazy.

Mr. Dalton was nice to Percy and Pauly, too, but he obviously had the best connection with me. I was really curious about his partner and their adopted girls. He had a photo on his desk of all of them sitting on a porch swing looking like a regular family you'd see anywhere except both the parents were men. I asked him if it was a lot of work raising twins. He smiled at me and said that I would know better than anyone. I told him I could babysit sometime if he wanted to have a night out with just him and his partner.

Sheryl put her arm around me and gave me a big squeeze into the side of her big breasts like she was real proud of me.

In the school hall were photographs of every graduating class. In one, I saw Mom there, smiling and wide-eyed. She looked really happy. She used to look like that sometimes while working with the women in the villages, but almost never when she was with Dad. Stretch's graduating class was two years before Mom's and therefore two picture frames over. He looked pretty much the same as he does now except he's got a few more wrinkles around his eyes and on his forehead. I'm sure he got those when his son died and his wife abandoned him. But his eyes looked happy and mischievous then, and they look pretty much the same now. Sheryl hasn't changed one bit since high school—though I didn't realize she was ten full years younger than Stretch. She looked happy and bouncy (if a little bit dumb) then and looks pretty much that way now. But I guess I've come to see that some people are smarter than they look.

If I didn't know what was really going on, I'd also guess for sure that she's had a boob job since high school, but that's not the case. Turns out, we're going to be having a baby around here in about five more months! We found out yesterday afternoon when Stretch called a "family meeting" in the living room. Percy tried to get out of it before it even started, but Stretch yelled at him and said if he didn't get into the living room right then, he was going to make Percy regret it. Sometimes, when Stretch yells, it's very intimidating.

Anyway, the meeting went like this:

Stretch: All right, everyone. Sheryl and I got some news for ya. (He looks at Sheryl, smiles, and then uses his thumb and his pointer finger to smooth his moustache.) You want to tell them, honey?
Me: (*Honey?* Gag.)
Sheryl: (Wearing a supershowy tank top and

259

smiling big.) Sure. Well, kids, we're going to have a baby!

Pauly: Whoa, cool!

June Bug: (Squealing and running to hug her mom.) I'm so happy for you!

Me: (Looking from Sheryl to Stretch with confusion.) What?

Percy: You mean, like, a real baby or an adopted one?

Stretch: (Reaching over and patting Sheryl's belly, which doesn't look pregnant yet.) Oh, it's a real one in there. Just like you were.

Me: (Staring at Sheryl's boobs and finally understanding that she hasn't been flaunting them around because she liked to. Understanding that she really couldn't help it. They were just growing and popping right out of everything she wore because she was pregnant.) Congratulations. (Deciding to put a little more emphasis into it, getting up, and going over to Stretch and hugging him.) Really, Uncle Stretch. (Looking up and seeing that his eyes are glistening, which make my own eyes start to glisten.) Congrats.

Pauly: Aw you cwying, Penny?

Percy: What a crybaby.

Sheryl: (Getting up and wrapping her arms around both Uncle Stretch and me, her boobs mashing into us, but me not even caring because I am so overwhelmed by tears of I don't know what. All kinds of feelings that are partly joy, partly sadness, partly relief, partly confusion, partly growing up, partly missing Mom, partly missing Dad, partly sad for Pauly, who will never know his natural mother, partly happy that Pauly has us, partly sad for the death of Roland, partly happy just seeing grumpy old Stretch looking so happy.) Penny's not a baby. We're very happy to share this with all of you kids. We love you. (Sheryl really gets on my nerves sometimes, but when she hugs you, you can really, really feel that she loves you.)

Stretch: And we're gettin' married come October.

June Bug and Pauly: (Screaming. Whooping. Jumping up and down.)

Me: (Still crying but then starting to laugh at the same time.)

Percy: Oh, I get it. Because of the baby.

Stretch: It's not just the baby, Son. I'd been tinkerin' with the idea of asking Sheryl to be my wife for a while now, before we got news of any baby comin'.

Percy: Can I name it?

Pauly: I don't think that's a vewy good idea.

Percy: Shut up, Pauly.

Despite Percy's childish comments, everyone

hugged and talked and shared their excitement for a while. It was a nice moment, and one of the first times I've felt "at home" anywhere in a long time. After we got done talking, Sheryl made an enjoyable dinner and we had rhubarb pie and ice cream and then all watched TV together.

It's hard to believe I get to be a bridesmaid! It's hard to believe Sheryl and Stretch are going to have a baby together! I thought Stretch was wayyyy past fatherhood age, but I guess not. Stretch and Sheryl said they're going to have the wedding on the farm. At first, I thought this was a *bad* idea (um, dirt, grime, and bad smells everywhere? On your wedding day?!). But the more I've thought about it, the more I've gotten used to it. Now it doesn't seem like that bad of an idea.

Even more than that, though, I'm superexcited for the baby. It's sorta like that baby belongs to all of us because when it's born, it'll be joining the family we already have here, and it won't know any better. Like, it won't know that I'm only its cousin or that Pauly's not even blood-related or that both its mom and dad had children with previous partners. It'll just think that Stretch, Sheryl, June Bug, Percy, Pauly, and me are its family. It won't even have to work to be part of its family. I'll just be its family automatically.

Dear Mom,

No, Percy did not save Jimmy's life from the tornado. Jimmy saved Percy's life. I don't know why he told you that he did the saving. Yes, it is wonderful that Percy did not get sucked up into a funnel cloud and flung halfway across the state of Minnesota. I am very happy for him.

Thanks for the money for new school clothes. Not that it matters, but how did you get money in jail? Anyway, I don't need much. June Bug and I have moved into the same bedroom to make room for a nursery and so we just kind of end up sharing clothes, too. It's all right. Though a lot of her things are yellow (?!), she has some nice stuff that isn't too tight or short or inappropriate. Best of all is she's pretty good to talk to about lots of things. She's not at all judgmental or anything. I can't stand people who are judgmental.

I'm really happy to hear that your appeal might go through, and you may only have a short time left to serve. I can't wait to have you back with Percy, Pauly, and me. And I think you're going to like living out here on the farm. I can't wait for us all to be together.

Penny

Dear Dad,

Percy did *not* save Jimmy's life from the tornado. Jimmy saved Percy's life. I don't know why Percy told you that he did the saving. Yes, we are all thankful that Percy survived the deadly, menacing, monstrous, chilling, humongous, frightful, terrible twister.

Well. I'm not surprised to hear about Peggy. I would've warned you if you'd asked for my opinion before you took up with her. But I'm sure you're hurting right now, and for that, I'm sorry. I think it would be really nice if you came and took us out for dinner. Just give us a call, and we'll be waiting for you. It's too bad that Peggy took all the money for the new church, but you've always been pretty good at finding ways to start up new churches, so maybe this is a blessing in disguise. You always said that the Lord works in mysterious ways.

One mysterious way that the world works is that I've had to abandon the list of banned books for the youth ministry program. I've read quite a few of them, and I have to say, they aren't at all wicked or evil. Some of them are pretty dumb and have thin plots and too many cliches, but those qualities don't make them sinful to read. Mostly, those books are a fun and exciting escape from the stresses of the real world. A lot of kids and even young women like myself need an occasional escape from their lives, even if it is with trifled, silly writing and not serious literature.

Sincerely,
Penny

Dear Jesus,

I should let you know up front that I haven't made up my mind about God or you, but I do believe that you lived and were a really good person. So on the merit of your speeches and amazing miracles that everyone says you did (though I'm not convinced), I want to talk to you about my brother Percy and thank you for saving him from the tornado, if you had anything to do with it. A lot of times, I act annoyed with Percy. He often bugs me, occasionally hurts me (both physically and emotionally), and he's not as good to talk to as I'd like him to be. But we've been through some trying times in the past year, and I'm pretty sure I'm spiritually closer to him than anyone else in the world. So if you *did* have anything to do with saving his life from the tornado, I'm really, really thankful. And even though I know he's probably going to do something *today* to bother me, like spy on me or say something really dumb or do something mean to Pauly that is going to permanently scar him, I would be truly devastated if he were not here.

Amen.

P.S. If you *are* real, and your father is real, why don't you just go talk to him and ask him to not send down any more tornadoes to Minnesota? If you would do that, it would probably be a lot easier for me to believe in you. Maybe you could send me a sign like the rainbow you sent to Noah after the ark and flood business was over. If not a rainbow, at least something definitely nonviolent. Do not send a plague!

TWO MONTHS Later . . .

Chapter 25
Percy the Survivor

Perseus Pribyl I Esq.
Descriptive Essay
Mr. Dalton's 8th Grade English

"How I Survived the Twister"

The deadly twister was large and in charge,
people. It looked like seven tornadoes in
one and it smelled like a dirt pie and it
tasted like a dirt sandwich and it sounded
like a scary band with lots of drums and it
felt like something bad. A bad storm. The
twister was deadly believe me all right?
First Jimmy who is really good at basketball and is a cool guy too was wearing this

really cool shirt with Bob Marley on it that day of the deadly twister. It was green and it smelled kind of bad and it looked very wrinkly but yours would too if you didn't fold it right when you put it in your bag before you took a trip. Trust me it was still cool. We were driving home from the state fair when all the sudden a cop made us go the wrong way at a traffic stop. A big cop so you had to listen. You might get a ticket if you don't listen or you might get thrown in jail. Stretch my uncle says it wasn't the cops fault but he sometimes blames the wrong person, believe me because I know about this kind of thing. Truly.

Secondly the deadly twister. All the sudden it came at us though you could barely see out the window anymore, just hold on I will get to that part. The deadly twister would of killed us easy if we would of kept on driving. No doubt. Jimmy said to me to get out of the car and run for yor "life!"! Or something like that I cannot remember exactly. He probably said to get out of the car "dude" and run for your life or something cool. He is always saying cool things like dude or something like that.

Next I was running for my life and the

deadly twister right behind, seriously believe me I was there. In a ditch we found shelter. From the deadly twister roaring overhead. Jimmy told me last week when we were talking about the deadly twister something he didn't tell me before which was something quite embarrassing. He took a crud in his pants! That is how scary this thing was! I didn't take a crud in my pants though.

Fourthly after the twister. It took a long time for us to look for Jimmy's car. We never did find it. We walked for a bunch of hours searching but there was nothing around except for a messed-up cow which I would of saved if I had time or a doctor's kit. We didn't even know where we were. It ticked off Jimmy that we could not find his car. He wasn't mad about the car because it is a bad automobile but he was mad about all these good CDs he had in there that he would have to reburn and also his guitar which flew who knows where. All I lost was a football which can be replaced and a duffel bag with some clothes in it. I don't even care about that. No big deal. We got picked up by this old guy in a truck who took us to a police station.

Fifth of all if anyone asks you police

stations are not scary take it from me. I have been to one so I can tell you for sure. Don't be frightened of them. They smell like garbage and they look scary but aren't and they sound normal just like a regular store except for a yell sometimes and they feel like a cold dungeon where you might get sent before you get your head chopped off in mid evil times and they don't taste like anything because you can't eat a jail. Seriously not too bad a place. Uncle Stretch came and got us from there and gave me a hug which he never did before.

Lastly they say there was fourteen tornadoes in Minnesota that day and eight poor people died. Not poor like they didn't have money but poor you know like I feel bad for them. But Jimmy and I weren't one of them!

In conclusion this descriptive essay was about me surviving the deadly twister! And Jimmy too he probably saved my life even though you could argue I saved his life in a way too since when I was holding onto his leg I was probably weighing him down just enough so he wouldn't get sucked up. I am 84 pounds. Imagine even trying to walk ten feet with an extra 84 pounds attached to your leg it would be hard.

I'm riding the bus home on a Friday. Pauly and Penny are sitting up front because nobody likes them that much yet. June Bug is sitting by her new boyfriend, Chad. He's not that great, but Penny says he's a gentleman. He seems boring to me, and he's got orange hair. I'm back with the cool kids, well, not *with* them but at least *by* them. I've got a couple of friends on a different bus, though. Tonight is Sheryl and Uncle Stretch's wedding. It's out at the farm, and we have to get all dressed up.

Today at school, I got my first A in English class for the essay on personal experience I wrote for Mr. Dalton's class. He's usually pretty picky, but he said just surviving that tornado to write about it was pretty much worth an A right there. Also, he said I did well by attempting to write creative similes and using sensory description. Everybody got to read their essays up front, and I got asked the most questions. Penny's essay was well-written and had a lot of words nobody's ever heard of, but I couldn't even tell you what it was about, it was so boring. One other kid nearly stole my idea when he wrote an essay about a tornado, but nobody asked him even one question, because his was more about his grandpa and the tornado, which was boring. A bunch of his grandpa's cows got killed when the barn collapsed was all that really happened. The kid wasn't even there. He was visiting his other grandpa in a different town where there weren't any tornadoes.

When the bus drops us off, the farmyard is an amazing sight. Flowers are hanging from all the trees and there's an altar and some chairs set up in the grass, with a big tent over them. When Uncle Stretch and Sheryl said they were getting married at the farm, I imagined it taking place in the barn with squealing pigs running around, and Uncle Stretch trying to look good in a suit but having crap on his shoes.

"It's beautiful!" says Penny.

"Weally awesome!" says Pauly.

I say, "It ain't that great."

Pauly says, "Whatevoh, P.P. Yoh just jealous."

"Jealous?" I say. "Of what? I'm not old enough to get married. I don't even want to get married."

We all walk up to the house. It's true—I don't want to get married, ever. Sheryl and Uncle Stretch both had failed relationships already, and look what happened to my parents' marriage. I like how things were in Africa. The men got to have two or three wives— sometimes more. There were these huge families and everybody seemed pretty happy. Probably because if the man of the house got in a fight with one of the wives, he'd just avoid her and hang out with a different one for a while.

When we get inside, Sheryl tells us we don't have

much time to get ready because the wedding starts at six. Her hair is all done up, and she actually looks very nice. Well, her belly looks a little weird, but that's because it's all poofed out since she's pregnant. She's been really nice to everyone lately. I mean, I guess she's always been nice, but now she's even trying to get Uncle Stretch to not be such a grouch to everyone, which I appreciate. It doesn't always work—like the time he kicked me in the butt and called me lazy last week because I forgot to mow the lawn when I was supposed to and then smarted off about it—but still, it's been better. Penny says Sheryl's nesting instinct is kicking in.

It takes a while, but finally, we're all dressed. I must say, I look good. I'm wearing a black suit with a red tie, and my hair is combed. Sheryl tried getting me to the dentist to fix my tooth, but I faked a stomachache that day, so I could stay cool looking with the broken tooth. After that, no one tried to schedule another dentist visit. As for Pauly, his suit is supposed to match mine, but he spilled some milk on it already, so I look better. Penny and June Bug are wearing these red dresses with ribbons all over them. Uncle Stretch wears a white tuxedo with black cowboy boots that don't have any crap on them, and he's actually shaved for once. Sheryl's dress is white, too, and it hides her gut, but her bosoms are kind of way out there.

Some guests show up, the ceremony starts, and we all stand up by the front: me and Pauly on one side, and Penny and June Bug on the other. Uncle Stretch stands up there next to us, waiting for Sheryl. There are more people invited to the wedding than I thought there'd be, but I don't know most of them since they're Uncle Stretch's and Sheryl's friends. Jimmy is here with his dad, though. He got a normal haircut and he's wearing a tie like most of the men. Still, he's got his earrings in his ears and his pierced eyebrow, so he still found a way to look cooler than everybody else.

I wish Mom were here. She told us her appeal went through, and she had a good chance to be released early from jail, early enough to even make the wedding, maybe. But I guess she couldn't make it. She would've been happy to see all of us so dressed up and looking good, and she probably would've been especially happy for Uncle Stretch, her brother.

I miss Dad, too, but in a different sort of way. If he were here, that would mean he would be the preacher, the guy marrying Uncle Stretch and Sheryl. He would probably say things that would make people nervous God was going to kill them if they didn't do what God wanted. People probably wouldn't want to be thinking about getting killed at a wedding. So I'm sort of glad he's not here. Still, I miss him.

Finally, Sheryl comes out of the house and walks

down the red carpet somebody rolled across the lawn. All the people in their seats stand up, and this person they hired to play a giant violin goes into some really loud stuff. This is good because Bernie and Brenda, who are tied to a tree, start whinnying—probably because they got scared. Though the music is loud, it sounds all right, and Sheryl is smiling like crazy as she walks down the carpet, holding some roses. They match the rose tattoo on her ankle, well, at least the part that's not tangled in barbed wire.

The ceremony doesn't last long. The most interesting part is when there's this man and woman, who look kind of like Uncle Stretch and Sheryl, who come up and do a song together. The guy has a really big red mustache and is wearing a leather vest with no shirt underneath, and he tonks on his guitar while the lady—who's got really big thingies and a yellow dress that barely covers them—sings along. They look and sound kind of weird, but their voices, though warbly and unnatural, somehow go together and make an interesting tune. And you can tell they're both trying really hard by the way they've shut their eyes so tight. The guy looks almost like somebody maybe knifed him.

Another interesting part is when Pauly is supposed to give the rings to the preacher, but when he digs in his pocket for them and pulls out his fist, all he's got cupped in his hand is a bunch of Starburst candy wrappers. The second time he digs in there, he pulls out the rings. I'm sure everybody was worried he'd lost them. I know I was, for a second. The rest is boring until the preacher announces, "You are now man and wife. Stretch, you may kiss the bride." Uncle Stretch is smiling like a little kid, smiling the biggest smile I've ever seen on his mean old face. Then he smooches her, and everybody claps, and it's done—they're married. The married couple gets on Brenda and rides a couple of laps around the farm while everybody hoots and hollers.

Afterwards, the party starts in the tent, and the weird-looking couple with the warbly voices plays the music. The guy unbuttons his leather vest and you can see his bare chest. He's got about ten curly chest hairs and a tattoo of a buffalo sitting there. He takes over the singing with a solo and all of a sudden the music sounds a lot worse. But the lady in the yellow dress kicks off her shoes and starts dancing, and other people copy her.

After a few songs, Sheryl comes up to me and tells me we're running low on punch and asks if Jimmy could take me to the store to buy some sherbet ice cream and ginger ale; she's already got the fruit juice. She says dinner starts in an hour, so would we hurry up, too? I go ask Jimmy, who's sitting at a table talking to this girl. He looks annoyed at first when he sees me but then says, okay, he'll do it, really nicely with a smile, probably just to impress the girl.

Penny sees me walking out with Jimmy and comes over. "Where are you going?" she asks.

"Gotta get some punch-bowl crap from the store for Sheryl," I say.

"Can I come along? This party is kind of getting weird."

I don't really want her to come, and Jimmy will probably be further annoyed, but I say, "I don't care. You have to ask Jimmy if we have enough room, though."

She smiles this awkward smile at him and stutters, "D-d-do you think I could come along for the ride?"

He looks at her funny and says, "Don't matter to me."

"Thanks," she says, and blushes. I suppose she's got a stupid crush on him! Great.

We get to Jimmy's vehicle. An old, beat-up truck has replaced his old, beat-up car that got whipped away in the tornado. We get in, Penny in the middle—to her delight, I'm sure—and Jimmy starts it up and loud music comes blaring. He turns it down a little.

When we get to the end of the driveway to make the turn into town, Jimmy has to wait for this little blue sports car coming at us. The blue car slows down as it gets closer and puts on its blinker. Probably some guests who got the time of the wedding wrong or something. The car turns into the driveway, and Jimmy starts to pull out. As we pass it, the blue car stops and the window rolls down, and Mom's face looks out. It's Mom.

It's Mom!

"Stop the truck!" I yell at Jimmy, jumping out even before he'd completely stopped. The only other time I moved so quickly was being chased by the tornado.

Penny's right behind me, and we jump on Mom when she gets out of the car. We're laughing and crying and jumping and screaming and hugging and kissing.

"Percy!" she says. "What happened to your front tooth?"

"Pauly kicked it out!" I say. "But I already forgave him."

"Oh, Lord," she says. "You'll have to tell me all about it."

I can't wait.

TWO MONTHS Later . . .

Chapter 26
Penny at Home

DEAR OKONKWO,

I AM ENCLOSING A FAMILY PHOTOGRAPH
ALONG WITH MY USUAL $5 THIS TIME. THAT'S
ME THERE IN THE LONG YELLOW DRESS NEXT
TO THE BOY WITH THE BIG SMILE WHO HAS
NO FRONT TOOTH. HE IS MY TWIN BROTHER,
PERCY.

I HEARD THAT IN SOME AFRICAN COUNTRIES,
PEOPLE USED TO ABANDON TWINS IN THE
WILDERNESS BECAUSE PEOPLE THOUGHT
MULTIPLE BIRTHS WERE ANIMAL-LIKE AND EVIL
AND DIDN'T WANT THE TWINS BRINGING DOWN
SOME BAD CHI ON THE TRIBE. I HATE TO BE THE
ONE TO BREAK IT TO YOU, BUT TWINS ARE NOT

EVIL AT ALL, SO I HOPE NO ONE DOES THAT IN YOUR COUNTRY ANYMORE.

TO TELL YOU THE TRUTH, MY TWIN AND I ARE SOME OF THE NICEST PEOPLE YOU COULD EVER HOPE TO KNOW. IN THE PICTURE, THE LITTLE TAN BOY IS MY BROTHER. HE IS ADOPTED, WHICH IS WHY WE DON'T LOOK LIKE THE SAME RACE. IN THIS COUNTRY, SIBLINGS ARE SOMETIMES DIFFERENT RACES BECAUSE ONE OF THEM MIGHT BE ADOPTED, BUT THEY COULD ALSO BE DIFFERENT RACES BECAUSE SOME MOMS HAVE KIDS FROM A COUPLE OF DIFFERENT MEN. THAT'S ONE OF THE GREAT THINGS ABOUT AMERICA. YOU CAN MAKE A FAMILY OUT OF ANY PEOPLE YOU WANT TO. SOME PEOPLE GET UPTIGHT ABOUT THE DISINTEGRATION OF THE NUCLEAR FAMILY, BUT I DON'T, AND YOU SHOULDN'T, EITHER.

WHEN YOU LOOK AT THE PHOTO OF MY FAMILY, BE SURE NOT TO CONFUSE ME WITH THE GIRL WITH THE FRENCH BRAID. THAT'S MY STEPCOUSIN, JUNE BUG, WHOM I DIDN'T LIKE AT FIRST BUT HAS BECOME PRETTY MUCH A SISTER TO ME. WE EVEN SHARE A ROOM. SHE'S STANDING NEXT TO HER MOM, SHERYL, WHO IS WEARING THE ROLLING STONES TANK TOP. SHE MARRIED MY UNCLE STRETCH, WHO'S IN THE

MIDDLE AND IS HOLDING THE BABY, CRITTER, WHOM EVERYBODY LOVES A LOT, AND NEXT TO HIM IS MY MOM. SHE'S GOT THE NICE SMILE.

I HOPE YOU FIND A FAMILY THAT IS AS SUPPORTIVE OF YOU AS I FEEL THE FAMILY IN THE PHOTO IS SUPPORTIVE OF ME. IF YOU DON'T, I DON'T MIND IF YOU THINK OF ME AS NOT JUST YOUR PEN "PAL" BUT YOUR PEN "SISTER."

YOUR CORRESPONDENCE MEANS A LOT TO ME, OKONKWO, AND I WISH YOU BLESSINGS UPON BLESSINGS.

YOUR PEN SISTER,

PENELOPE PRIBYL

Dear Diary,

This house is really small. There are only three rooms plus a bathroom on the first floor. There are two big bedrooms and two small bedrooms on the second floor. There is one bedroom in the attic and there's a rec-room-type thing in the basement if you can stand centipedes and spiders. Stretch and Sheryl get one room, Baby Jessalyn (whom everybody has started calling Critter) gets a room, Pauly gets a room, and June Bug and I share a room. Mom has the attic bedroom, which gets really hot, but she says she is used to heat and doesn't mind. And Percy, who's finally opened up to the idea of seeing the dentist about his tooth, still sleeps in the granary. We all share one TV, which still only gets ten channels and which Sheryl still hogs all day especially since now that she's just sitting around, constantly nursing the baby day and night. Critter eats a lot! She is already about five pounds overweight, in my opinion.

I've never minded being in overcrowded, small places. I actually kind of like them. You never get lonely. Yes, you have to give up some privacy, but if you're careful and don't dance around naked, it's no problem.

Having Mom around again has made me realize how much I missed her and how much my brothers needed her. Mom always has the right thing to say to people. I really want to be like that someday, too, but I think it's a talent and something you're born with, and I don't know if I have it or not. Stretch has really livened up with Mom around. They have all these old inside jokes and sayings, which I can't imagine Percy and I ever having together. Well, except for *Horse Camp*, I guess.

Since she won her appeal, Mom has taken up golf (?!), plays in a horseshoes league (?!) every Tuesday night in town, and is doing a lot of reading and is thinking of getting into politics, believe it or not. She says our government is only as good as the people who make it up, and to prove it, she's volunteering for our local representative, who used to be her teacher in high school. She's been telling me what bozos Minnesota has had for some of its leaders in the last decade or so, and I wouldn't doubt if she ends up running for an office herself someday. She's one of those people who could probably do about any job.

Willy (Wesley's dad) is Mom's new boyfriend, or actually, *old* boyfriend since it turns out they used to date way back in sixth grade, which Mom just told me the other day. (She tends to save really important pieces of information for too long in her mind, which makes it seem like the things she does are crazy until she lets you in on the important stuff. I wonder how many other things she hasn't told me.) Since I broke up with Wesley, I don't mind Mom dating Willy.

Wesley and I agreed that we were better suited to be friends, since he's planning on living on his farm for his whole life, and I have big plans about studying abroad and learning French. I can't do those things on a farm.

Dad has moved back to the area and has begun showing up randomly to pick us up for visits, but then he ends up hovering around here, which bothers Uncle Stretch and Willy. Legally, Dad has only custodial rights to see us every other weekend, but until everyone gets used to the new way of life around here, we're trying to be accepting of any efforts he makes.

He is our dad and I love him, of course, but mostly I feel sorry for him because now he's all alone. His new church on the Internet is growing very quickly, with lots of new parishioners joining all the time, and he loves recording his sermons and posting them on his Web site, rather than having to spend all that time in a church or traveling to random spots around the globe.

I've got to hand it to Dad. He knows how to draw a crowd and keep things moving, and I'm especially amazed at how savvy he is on a computer when so many other adults these days have just given up on technology and don't want to have anything to do with it. But something I'm *not* proud of him for is the way he seems to have trouble remembering that he's not married to Mom anymore and that she can date whomever she wants.

He keeps telling us things like fornication is a sin, and divorce is a sin, and that he built the new church on the Internet for Mom, who acts like she doesn't even appreciate it. I, for one, know that Mom *doesn't* appreciate it and has no intention of ever caring for his ministry again, but he just doesn't get it. I, for one, happen to remember that Dad initiated the divorce. I can see that he is now reshaping and misremembering events because he regrets the way things turned out. He doesn't realize that he'll feel better when he accepts the changes in his life and moves forward.

Now that I'm older, I can see that Dad's just really insecure, so I have been trying to think of ways to let him know that it's okay for him to just be himself when he's with me and that he doesn't have to impress me or anyone else by making big speeches in front of lots of people. I don't mind if he comes around, because if I were him, I'd want to be around all of us, too, but I'm not sure Willy feels quite so generous. So sometimes if I know Dad's coming, I'll act like I'm really exasperated with hanging out on the farm and ready to leave, and then he'll take me (and sometimes Percy and Pauly) out somewhere.

Last week, he showed great improvement by agreeing to just go running for a couple of miles with Percy and me. Running is a new hobby of mine, a great way to stay healthy and commune with the universe at the same time, and it's a good opportunity to spend time with Percy in a way that isn't annoying, except that I have to listen to him talk about training for the NFL all the while. The first mile, Dad was talking and talking and talking, but after we passed Rabbit River, he stopped blabbing because he was tired and ran out of breath, and that's when the best part of the run began to take place.

When his voice stopped, all of a sudden I could hear the sounds our shoes made when they hit the gravel, and the sounds we made when we inhaled and exhaled (especially Dad). I also heard the sounds of a far-off tractor in a field and the grass swaying in a ditch, and I noticed how bright and lush the green crops in the fields looked, and I felt myself sweating and busy and warm inside as my legs carried me along. We all turned around at the two-mile mark and started running back to the farm. Dad fell back, but he waved Percy and me on ahead of him. We kept up our pace, nice and easy at first. We jogged and pumped our arms in a common rhythm, and I thought about those months we spent together in Mom's womb and the months we survived together at Uncle Stretch's farm. I thought about how when Critter was born, Uncle Stretch took us all to the hospital to see her. I thought about the photo we took with me holding Critter, Uncle Stretch holding Pauly, and June Bug and Percy sitting on the bed with Sheryl. I thought about coming down the stairs one night and finding Uncle Stretch walking the floor with Critter on his shoulder, humming a little song to her that I remembered Mom singing to Pauly when he was little.

I thought about how sometimes Percy's going one way, and I'm going the other. I thought about how different we are and how similar. Then I pushed myself a little harder, ran a little faster. Then Percy strode a little higher and ran a little faster. The pebbles kicked up beneath our feet. We each panted for air. Percy got out ahead of me a couple of inches. I willed my legs to go faster. I could feel my chest getting tighter. Dad shouted, "Go, kids, go!" And we did. We ran. We competed. We raced toward the farm, pushing ourselves, pushing each other all the way home.

Acknowledgments

The authors wish to thank . . .

Isabella, Mitchell, and Phillip, for being who they are and doing what they do.

The influences of our fathers, mothers, sibs, cousins, aunts, uncles, and grandparents.

The Wednesday Writers of Mankato.

Agent Faye Bender.

Ruth Katcher and Egmont USA.

Our junior high English teachers: Mr. Bob Rise and Mrs. Julie Neubauer.

Edgar Allan Poe and Victor Hugo.

The compassion of Elle MacPherson.

Ernest Hemingway and Scott Fitzgerald.

Damien Lods.

The many peoples and animals of the state of Minnesota.

The students and teachers and vibe of Mankato State University's MFA Program circa the early 2000s.

Ngugi wa Thiongo, Bapsi Sidwa, Mark Richard, Denis Johnson.

The Little Three: Violette, Archibald, and Gordon.

Camp Dells.

All our friends.

Each other.

Horses everywhere.